"What are you, Cade?"

"I'm just a man, Sienna." That much was true. He couldn't lose her yet, couldn't lose her to fear. He still needed her help to find the *Santa Josefa*. Needed her trapped memories.

"You're not a man. Men can't breathe underwater without a tank. You didn't need a tank. You didn't need *anything*. You—" She backed up as he kept coming toward her. "Last night in the lagoon. You kissed me. You breathed air into my lungs!"

It was too late to deny it.

"You don't have to be afraid of me, Sienna. I'm not going to hurt you."

He took a chance and reached out to touch her. Just the barest skim of his finger against her face and he could feel the shivering of her entire body.

"I'm still a man, Sienna. I'm human, just like you."

Dear Reader,

There is nothing more tantalizing and romantic than lost treasure. The so-called "treasure fleet" of Spanish galleons sailing the seas off the Americas left a trail of sunken gold that has inspired dreams and adventures for hundreds of years and got me thinking.... What if amid the pieces of eight, silver bars and jeweled rings a secret lay that could blow up the eastern seaboard? And then I thought, who could possibly combat undersea terrorism but one hot and sexy merman from the PAX League?

Join PAX superagent Cade Brock and Sienna Parker, an unsuspecting former treasure hunter who finds herself in the wrong place at the wrong time, as they work to uncover an ancient threatening secret before it's too late for the world... and their hearts.

I hope you have as much fun reading *Deep Blue* as I had writing it!

Love,

Suzanne McMinn

Suzanne McMinn

Deep Blue

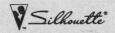

Silhouette®

INTIMATE MOMENTS™

Published by Silhouette Books

America's Publisher of Contemporary Romance

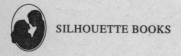 SILHOUETTE BOOKS

ISBN 0-373-27475-0

DEEP BLUE

Copyright © 2006 by Suzanne McMinn

All rights reserved. Except for use in any review, the reproduction or utilization of this work in whole or in part in any form by any electronic, mechanical or other means, now known or hereafter invented, including xerography, photocopying and recording, or in any information storage or retrieval system, is forbidden without the written permission of the editorial office, Silhouette Books, 233 Broadway, New York, NY 10279 U.S.A.

All characters in this book have no existence outside the imagination of the author and have no relation whatsoever to anyone bearing the same name or names. They are not even distantly inspired by any individual known or unknown to the author, and all incidents are pure invention.

This edition published by arrangement with Harlequin Books S.A.

® and TM are trademarks of Harlequin Books S.A., used under license. Trademarks indicated with ® are registered in the United States Patent and Trademark Office, the Canadian Trade Marks Office and in other countries.

Visit Silhouette Books at www.eHarlequin.com

Printed in U.S.A.

SUZANNE McMINN

lives by the lake in North Carolina with her husband and three kids, plus a bunch of dogs, cats and ducks. Visit her Web site at www.SuzanneMcMinn.com to learn more about her books, newsletter and contests. Check out www.paxleague.com for news, info and fun bonus features connected to her "PAX league" series about paranormal superagents!

Chapter 1

Cade Brock lowered the binoculars he had trained on the house down the street, his grip tightening on the cell phone at his ear as his pulse froze. "What did you say?"

The PAX League chief, Harrison Beck, let a beat draw out. "It's Adal Chaba. I wanted to tell you myself."

"Keep going." Cade continued to watch the target location from the parked car he'd positioned down the block even as his jaw clenched and something dark banded his chest.

"We nailed Kerbasi," Beck told him. "We got

the data off his hard drive that links him to Chaba. I'm taking you off the case."

"No." The word burst tightly out of Cade's mouth. His fingers moved of their own accord to the rigid slice of a scar not four weeks old on the side of his throat. A parting gift from Harmon Kerbasi. If he hadn't wanted this case for revenge already, knowing Kerbasi was linked to the terrorist kingpin Chaba clinched it.

"You sound like hell," Beck said. "As much as we need you on this case, it's too soon. This is too personal already, and now—"

"No." He knew he sounded like hell. He felt like hell. But he had people to *put* in hell. And yeah, it was personal. "You need me."

"You need some R&R."

"I had enough R&R." The last month, in the hospital then recovering at home on enforced leave, had been more R&R than he'd ever wanted or intended to suffer again. He needed a case to work on. Downtime was nothing but an invitation to nightmares of guilt and loss so deep he didn't want to relive them. And yet he did. Every time he closed his eyes. And sometimes when they were open.

"You need to come in for more testing."

He was sick and tired of testing. And he knew the PAX chief didn't just mean the endless scientific probing he'd endured for most of his life. Beck meant psychological testing. He knew what they thought of him. They called him "The Machine" as if he weren't even human. And maybe he gave that impression. Good enough. He didn't have buddies in the League. He worked alone, no other agents at his side. He liked it that way. If they thought that made him an emotionless machine, so be it. He was respected but not befriended. He kept his emotional distance. It was better for everyone that way. Especially him.

Changing any of that wasn't on his agenda.

"I'm not coming in for more testing. I'm not going back on R&R. And you can take me off the case, but I'm not taking myself off." He had a slippery relationship with the League. Technically, he was their agent. They'd raised him from age six, and some people would say that made them his family. But they'd never owned him, and the last thing they were going to do when it came to Chaba was control him. "Now tell me about Chaba."

Another moment passed in which he was certain Beck was considering the ten different ways he wanted to throttle him. The PAX chief respected him, though, and he knew what getting Chaba meant to Cade.

"The hard drive didn't have much on it," Beck said finally. "Kerbasi'd been ditching his laptop

regularly. Chaba's careful. He would have insist-
ed on that. Unless Kerbasi starts talking, all we've
got are a few e-mails that link him up the chain of
command. We need the woman. She's the key."

A red compact car slid down the street toward
the house and stopped. Tall and leggy, the woman
stepped out of the car then turned to scan the quiet, palm-lined Key Mango street. Cade lifted the
binoculars again.

"And I've got her," he said.

He punched the phone off, leaving the PAX
chief without the time, or the connection, to
change one damn thing that was about to happen.
Cade watched the target stand, rooted, for a few
moments in the driveway of the house.

It was almost too convenient. Not even a challenge. It couldn't have been easier if she'd tied a
ribbon around her slim, pretty neck and handed
herself to him.

He waited, adrenaline burning, in the nonde-
script sedan he'd rented, parked several houses
down and across the street from the two-story
house. There was an apartment on bottom, another on top. Nothing was this easy, and he wasn't
taking any chances. He'd tangled with Tabitha
Donovan before, and she'd nearly cost him his
life when she'd left him to Kerbasi. There would
be no repeats of that scenario.

She stood there, as if she were waiting for someone, too, as he'd been waiting for her. Or did she fear someone was after her? For a second, he thought she was going to get back in the car and drive away. If someone *was* after her—someone besides him—well, he might have a chance to kill two birds with one stone, because the people she was dealing with were even more elusive than Tabitha Donovan—or whatever she was calling herself today. And they were definitely a hell of a lot more dangerous.

Cade knew from personal experience that mass murder was Chaba's stock in trade.

"Run, baby. Run!"

His mother's wild eyes seared him as he wobbled, panicked, on the fiery beach.

"Take care of your brother. You're a big boy."

"No, Mama." He clung to her arm even as she pushed him away.

"I have to find your father, baby. Take your brother. Run!"

She shook him off, and turned….

Fire, then blackness and screaming, so much screaming—

Cade squeezed his eyes shut for a horrific beat. For the millionth time, he couldn't stop the screaming, couldn't go back and make it different, couldn't change the lives that had been lost, couldn't bury the memories and anger deep enough. Even blowing Chaba to hell wouldn't do that. But it would be a start.

He opened his eyes and focused on the present, the woman, the link to the evil that had haunted him all his life.

Even from a distance in the clouded twilight, she was the most gorgeous terrorist he'd ever seen. She wore hip-hugging pink cropped pants and a white camisole top that clung to curvy breasts and a trim waist. Blond hair fell free to her shoulders, and even in the soggy Florida Keys heat, she looked fresh as the proverbial daisy.

He tipped the binoculars to his eyes—the better to see her deceptively lovely oval face in the scant light, slender with intriguing hollows that made her look delicate…when she was anything but.

She nibbled her lip as she hesitated in front of the building. Did she see him, even from this distance, through the tinted windows and murky shadows of the oncoming night and a brewing storm?

A breeze whipped the lush palm fronds up and down the street and the first plops of the storm front hanging gray in the sky above hit his windshield. She turned to retrieve an overnight bag from the rear of the vehicle. She hadn't seen him. She didn't have a clue.

She was about to get one.

He lowered the binoculars, satisfied. She'd be

spending the rest of her life in a government lock-up if what the PAX League believed about her was true. And considering the evidence he had already, he didn't have any doubts. In the meantime, they needed her.

Alive, not dead, and with the dangerous double-crossing game she was playing, she was on borrowed time already. She didn't know it, but he was about to save her sorry life.

Getting to the truth, and to her secrets, including her real identity, was his job, and unfortunately, that meant keeping her alive. He watched as she swayed her wickedly sexy hips, crossing to the wooden outside steps leading up to the second-story apartment, overnight bag in hand. The small island community of Key Mango that she'd apparently chosen for her home base was hardly exclusive housing. The tiny key was made up primarily of locals, shrimp trawling seamen and dive fanatics, with a sprinkling of Bahamian rental homes and run-down duplex apartments that attracted tourists going for economical over trendy. Not that anything came cheap down here. Even a one-bedroom weather-beaten studio on the least fashionable island in the coral keys would cost a pretty penny this close to the water.

Tabitha Donovan had plenty of pretty pennies tucked in her secret Swiss bank account, no doubt courtesy of Chaba, but she wasn't showing them off, not with the used car she was driving and not with the less than stellar housing she'd used a credit card in her made-up name to lease. It was how PAX had tracked her here. Mistakes. Criminals always made them, even the beautiful ones.

The street lay quiet in the early evening, nothing but the beat of palm fronds in the wind and the rush of gathering rain hitting the steaming street. This late in the summer, the vacation renters were heading out and more than half the homes and apartments were empty, their distant owners putting months at a time on sale to attract off-season travelers who would be arriving in the coming weeks. The cute blonde wasn't planning to leave, though. She'd booked her rental through the fall. The better to search for the ancient secret she was planning to sell out at the cost of thousands, maybe hundreds of thousands, of lives.

But her plans were about to change. Whether he liked it or not—and he didn't—she was going with him, and going alive. She was a pawn on his way to the top, and now that he knew that top was Chaba, he'd do anything to get there. Even put up with the woman who'd set him up to die.

Shiny hair tucked behind one ear, she pushed the key in the lock of the upstairs apartment. He debated his options. Was the lower level of the building occupied? There were no lights, no signs of life from the first floor residence, but a van was parked on the street in front of the building. He'd been watching for nearly an hour. He didn't want any hassles with nosy neighbors interfering if she started screaming bloody murder. No way was he letting her, possessor of the deadly secrets of the *Santa Josefa* and his link to Chaba, slip away, and no way would she go with him easily.

She thought he was Cade Brock, renegade treasure hunter, playboy, wastrel, only interested in the lost Spanish shipwreck for his own gain. It was a role he played well. Just as well as she played Tabitha Donovan. He absently fingered the scar at his throat. He wasn't interested in money at all, though he had an amazing knack for acquiring it. He wanted justice. And oh yeah, revenge. He was a PAX agent, but no matter what his fellow agents thought of him, he was also a man, human despite the physiological mutations that made him of unique value to the League.

Through the uncurtained upper-story window, he watched the woman walk into the apartment, shut the door and shove something—the car key?—into her back pocket and then… A shadow moved from behind the door as she shut it. A shadow that reached for her throat and yanked her back into his arms.

Cade's pulse slammed and he keyed the ignition. He wasn't the only one who'd been waiting for Tabitha Donovan. And this had just stopped being easy.

She tasted panic and pain as a hard arm appeared out of nowhere, slamming her back against an even harder body. Her overnight bag thunked to the floor. A scream strangled in her throat as the pressure of the hand over her face left her desperate for air.

Spots swam in her vision. The shadows of the apartment faded toward black.

Adrenaline surged past the shock and fear. The attacker's hand moved slightly. She could breathe through her nose and her vision cleared. The chilling butt of a gun pressed against her temple.

Was this what had happened to Sabrina? Or did he think *she* was Sabrina?

Sabrina with her strange disappearances, her mysterious plans, the charts in her apartment— Not that she'd wanted to believe any of that. Not that Sienna had wanted to believe her twin sister was doing what she thought she was doing.

Sabrina had also mentioned she was involved with a man, a man who frightened her, and now… Desperate, Sienna twisted her head, managed to break free of the hand over her mouth for a second.

"This isn't what you think," she said quickly, her voice thin, unrecognizable. "I'm not Sa—"

The hand brutally retook her mouth and she couldn't breathe again.

"Shut up and pick that bag back up then open the door," a rough voice ordered in her ear. "Walk outside. Slowly."

She had to get away. She'd open the door, and then she'd make a break for it. She'd run. She'd scream. But for now, she could barely feel her shaking hand as she picked up the bag then reached for the knob with her other hand, pulling open the door of her sister's shadowed apartment.

Fear left her swimming in a disembodied, surreal state in which she just knew this couldn't be happening to her. This happened to women she heard about on the news. Choppy, disjointed sound bites of women abducted and murdered staggered wildly through her mind.

The rain-laced breeze struck her as the man pushed her onto the small landing. He was right behind her.

"Move," the attacker demanded, and she did.

She twisted in his arms, shot her knee into his groin and, in the split instant when he roared, she ripped away from him, still gasping for breath, stumbling blindly down the steps.

Pain exploded as he grabbed her back and slammed the gun against the side of her head, choking her scream. Her bag thunked down the stairs, rolling to a stop.

The blow brought tears stinging to her eyes and then she forgot pain, forgot everything except the deadly coldness of the eyes she saw as the man ripped her to her feet and jerked her tightly against him again. She was aware of hollowed features, dark clothes, iron strength. Rain dashed against his cheeks, sliding down as if off a slab of marble.

"Don't do that again." He jerked her around, pushing her down the rest of the stairs ahead of him.

Horror gripped her as she realized the van parked on the street in front of the apartment must be his. He pushed her toward it. He was going to take her away from here and do God knows what to her next. All she knew about crimes against women told her that if she got in that van, she was going to die.

Another man pushed out of the rear passenger sliding door of the van suddenly. Another man with another gun. He dashed forward, grabbed her bag and threw it in the van before turning back. Why were they taking it? Her mind reeled. There was still the rental car. When Sabrina got here, she'd find it, know she'd been here... But it would be too late.

"Get in the van," the attacker snarled, releasing

her to propel her forward toward the other man, and she caught the tip of her sandal in a break in the cement walk.

She fell to the wet concrete, hitting her knees, the impact robbing her of breath or she'd be screaming. She lifted her eyes as the man grabbed her by her hair and a dark movement flashed into her consciousness even as new pain seared her head.

"You're lucky he doesn't want you dead," he snarled. "Yet."

He? Who was *he?*

A screech of tires broke the wind-whipped air. Rain splattered down, harder now, as a dark sedan swung to a halt in the middle of the street. A man reared from the car, leaning over the hood, a dark object glinting in his hand. Police?

Her heart thudded against her ribs. No. Like the men abducting her, he was dressed in civilian clothes, a black T-shirt stretched over powerful shoulders. Clipped brown hair, lean-planed features, chilling eyes.

And a gun.

Rain instantly plastered his hair to his head as the drops turned into a downpour.

"Let her go," he shouted.

The hand holding her shoved her sideways and she was back on her knees as the sound of gunfire exploded. She heard the distant sound of a door opening down the street, a startled scream, then a slam.

She realized one of the men was down, the man who'd jumped out of the van. Blood.

Her pulse boomed in her ears. She scrambled on her hands and knees for the red compact car she'd rented at the airport in Key West, pulling the door open and banging inside, desperate breaths biting her lungs. She felt the humid warmth of the leather seat, her clothes and hair dripping onto it.

Adrenaline burned her veins and she could barely think. *The key.*

She twisted awkwardly, shoving her hand into her back pocket. Was it there or had she dropped it in the apartment when he'd grabbed her?

Heart thumping into her throat, her fingers closed with numbed panic over the cold outline of the rental car key.

Whipping her head to the window, she could barely see the outline of the man who'd grabbed her in the apartment. He'd made it to cover behind his van and another shot boomed through the pounding rain as he aimed at the man crouched behind the sedan.

Surely the police would be on the way. But how long would it take them to get here? Did tiny

Key Mango even *have* full-time emergency personnel?

One of the two men left was going to kill the other, and then they'd come for her. And the idea that at least one of them had sworn he didn't want her dead, *yet*, wasn't a comfort.

And as for the other one...

He looked every ounce as dangerous as the abductor and he'd just shot a man dead. They were fighting over her—or fighting over Sabrina, if that's who they thought she was. *Why?* Where was Sabrina?

Panic roared through her bloodstream. She slammed the key in the ignition and sobbed when the car leaped to life. She screeched backward, plowing past the man by the sedan, striking the fender. A flash of hot blue eyes seared her as he reared back out of her way.

She braked, spun, and in the stormy blur of the rearview mirror as she floored it, she saw the abductor from the apartment seize the moment of distraction to make it around his car and leap into the van. He was coming after her!

Town. She had to head back to town. Find people. Key Mango didn't have much, but she'd driven past a commercial strip of businesses, restaurants, small neighborhoods and a church, before reaching the touristy outskirts of beach rentals. She gulped in panicked breaths, roaring at blinding speed through the tearing rain.

And she didn't have the slightest idea where she was going. Had she missed the turn back toward the town?

All she could see on either side of the road were jungle-thick mangroves. She'd gone into the interior of the island, but this wasn't the road to town. Desperation clawed at her stomach. She crossed a bridge fanning over a lagoon. She must have gone the wrong way from the beginning.

Headlights broke the storm-dark behind her. She caught a sign whizzing past: Key Mango Bird Sanctuary. Ahead, through the rain, she saw a chain-link fence, the gate padlocked shut. Dead end.

The car spun, sliding sideways, tires losing traction on the wet road. She regained control and headed back, whipping past the van as it, too, spun around.

As she hit the bridge again, she saw the sedan coming straight at her. She jerked the wheel to swerve around it. She should never have left North Carolina. *This was a nightmare. This couldn't be happening. She was a university librarian. She never did anything more risky than exceed the daily recommended fat intake for a woman of her height and weight.*

That was the last thought she had before she realized the car was hydroplaning. She felt the bizarre sensation of spinning over the blacktop road, then the shocking crash of breaking through the guardrail.

Dark water slammed up at her—oh, God, water!—and she struck the windshield.

Chapter 2

Cade hit the brakes, hanging on to the wheel as the sedan threatened to twist into a dangerous spin, stopping only when he crashed into the van that ground to a stop just short of following the woman's car through the wiped-out guard rail. The impact thunked him forward hard, then back, his seat belt holding him in place.

He jumped out, tearing through the howling wind and slashing rain. The driver of the van lay against the steering wheel, blood pouring out of the side of his head.

The man moved, mumbled, his eyes flashing

open. Cade landed his fist into the man's face and he slammed back, dead to the world again.

Cade raced from the van to the edge of the bridge and dove straight in. No way was he losing his target—and the lagoon was about to swallow her whole. The passenger compartment was taking in water fast. Already, the car was more than halfway to a watery grave. His body, skin made up of microdermal ridges invisible to the naked eye, streamed into the dark water like another liquid.

He'd been six years old when his adoptive parents had found him at the bottom of the family swimming pool. They'd thought he was dead. He was just napping, and the fact that everyone didn't nap underwater was news to him.

The PAX League had already discovered that a shocking number of the children who'd survived the Valuatu Island bombing several years earlier had returned home with strange aftereffects. Biological mutations. And thus, the PAX League, once an organization dedicated purely to the philosophical pursuit of global peace through human rights missions, environmental campaigns and charitable projects such as the Valuatu Island hunger delegation, had transformed into something more.

Beginning with those children, the new and secret underlayer of Paranormal Allied Experts had spent years researching the mystical, telepathic and transformational sciences. Its goal was not only to protect the work of the League's outer humanitarian organization, but to prevent terror worldwide as it molded those original children into agents and created even more through its own experimentation.

And Cade had lost his family—again.

He surged back up to the surface beside the car, not for air—he didn't need it. But she did. The woman's head slumped against the window, water rising to her neck. He saw tangled wet hair, blood. Bracing his feet against the side of the vehicle, he yanked at the door.

The water reached her mouth and nose and he slipped beneath the surface now to pull at the door. He saw the woman gasp and jerk back as the lack of oxygen stabbed her into consciousness.

With corneas and lenses shaped to see light through water, he had the visibility to see her eyes bulge as she first jerked up to take in air, then reached for the door handle. She shoved uselessly, then screamed, taking in water again, and pushed up to the interior roof of the car, coughing and gagging, struggling for the last few inches of air.

Then she slid her head sideways, panic in her gaze as she met his through the water. She was in emotional shock, had been even before the crash, and the physical shock was going to set in fast. The lagoon wasn't cold, but without the specialized thermoregulatory system that kept him warm, she was probably losing body temperature already and at the rate the car was sinking, she'd be out of air in less than a minute if he didn't get the door open.

Still underwater, he motioned in efficient movements for her to shove as he pulled. Her gaze flicked down then back to his face as the water crept higher.

Fear and survival warred in her eyes.

No two ways about it, she was scared of anyone who would have leaped off that bridge after her.

He grabbed the handle, yanked hard. The pressure of water inside and outside the car held it firm. He felt his muscles bunching as he heaved on the handle again.

The water completely covered the car now and it was sinking at accelerated speed. He could see her holding one last breath of air, anxiously pushing outward against the door even as he pulled. The lagoon wasn't deep, twenty or thirty feet, he estimated, and the car tumbled heavily now to the bottom, sand clouding upward from the disturbed bottom. He didn't need more air, but she did, and soon.

One more heaving pull, and the car door suddenly thrust outward. Reaching blindly through the muddied water, he felt her soft, drenched body.

He pushed hard with his feet against the sand of the lagoon floor and streamed upward toward the clear surface and the light of the storm. She felt like nothing in his arms. He gave a last powerful kick, popping up to the surface. He shifted to grip her tightly against his heat with one arm as he swam.

Pulling her up on the damp, sandy shore, he felt her react, coughing and gagging as she had in the car. He set her down and she rolled over, retching.

Rain lashed down. He was stunned for a second by how glad he was that she was alive. The helpless panic in her eyes when the car filled with water… The memory of it streaked into him. In the dim light he watched her shoulders tremble, and she turned, lifting her pale, shocked gaze to his.

For a long moment the storm seemed to almost recede around them, and then she pushed herself up on her elbows. In spite of himself, he felt something strange and unallowable. Sympathy.

He shoved it back. She didn't deserve it.

He'd been tricked by her once, and he wouldn't be tricked again.

He stood over her, water streaming down his sides. "You're coming with me."

"No," she gasped, barely audible over the pounding rain. "No."

She scrambled away. He tore up the bank, twisting her and pinning her on her back where she fell against the soggy ground.

"Stop!" he ordered.

"No!" she screamed. "Let me go!"

Her eyes were huge, shocked, radiating cold fear. He could feel the trembling of her body, see the confusion in her wild eyes. He held on, even as she struggled. She felt different than he expected.

Lighter, softer somehow.

Raindrops slid down his face and onto hers. Her breaths came in panting gasps. The storm blew around them.

"Not this time," he grated, his voice whipped away in the wind. He jerked her to her feet. "You're not getting away this time."

"I don't know what you're talking about!"

"You know exactly what I'm talking about, Tabitha."

"I'm not Tabitha!" she shouted at him. "I'm Sienna!" Inches away, her eyes were lost and scared, and her words knocked him off balance enough that she was able to tear free again and run, slipping and sliding, up the bank.

He made chase, and she didn't have a chance. Together they slammed into the drenched, sandy bank.

A shocked breath escaped her, then she was fighting him again, shoving against him with her hands. He grabbed both arms and pinned them to her sides, covering her body with his.

"My name is Sienna!" she cried. "Whoever you want, I'm not her! That was my sister's apartment. My twin sister. Sabrina. I don't know who Tabitha is!"

He felt something icy prick at the back of his neck. He sensed the shaking desperation of her body, knew the piercing confusion of her gaze.

She was a liar. She had lied to him before. She'd lie to him again. It was all he could do not to shake the truth out of her right there and then on the bank of the storm-tossed lagoon, but—

"Nobody said anything about a sister." He gripped her arms tighter when she tried to get away. She contorted her body as she struggled to free herself. He could feel her heart pounding against him as she turned her wild gaze back to him.

"Well, I'm saying something about it! I'm not Sabrina," she cried. "Or Tabitha! I don't know who those men were at the apartment. I don't know who you are! I'm telling you the truth."

"You wouldn't know the truth if it bit you in the ass," he ground back at her. "Sabrina. Tabitha. Whatever you're calling yourself today." Fury rose up again.

"Sienna. My name is Sienna!"

A sound pricked his hearing through the wind and the rain. He lifted his head. Someone was coming up the road. Headlights swayed through the storm above them on the bridge. A car door slammed.

She pushed against him again. "Police—"

He cut his gaze back to the woman beneath him, let go of one of her arms and wrapped his hand over her mouth. Before she could try anything else, with his other arm, he forcibly rolled her over him, down the bank, his body thunking against the ground, against her, once, twice, till they were up against the foot of the bridge.

Voices sounded above them, the words carried away by the wind. Then a gunshot exploded, and seconds later a body flew darkly past them, over the bridge and into the water.

Whoever the hell was up on that bridge, it wasn't the police. Whoever it was had just executed the man from the van and dumped his body right in front of them.

Close against his chest, the woman's gaze spun,

locked with his. She was so close, he could feel every panicked beat of her heart.

Then, more voices, shouts, and they were coming closer, down off the bridge.

They were coming to see if there was anyone left alive down here. He could see the understanding streak across the woman's shocked eyes. He could see the battle as she decided who was more dangerous—them or him.

"I'm going to take my hand off your mouth," he said quietly, quickly. "And you're going to get back in the water."

"I can't." Her voice was thin, begging. She wasn't fighting him now. She wasn't moving, period. He yanked her to her feet.

"You can." He slipped to the bank, pulled her with him. They had no more than seconds before they'd be seen. "Or they'll kill you."

"And you won't?"

Vengeance twisted, sharp in his gut. Kill her? God, he'd like to. "No."

"I can't swim!" she shrieked, and in the same second he shoved her in, he realized he had no idea who the hell she was.

Because she wasn't lying. She couldn't swim. *She wasn't Tabitha Donovan.*

Chapter 3

The water was dark, swirling with shadows and one big, fearsomely powerful man. Sienna felt light and heavy, panic and shock so familiar now. A nightmare that would never end, that's what she was living.

Crazy strangers with guns above.

Crazy stranger holding her captive below.

Below water.

She was going to die. She was going to drown. *He was drowning her.* And she was going to have a full-blown panic attack. No way could she think straight. She felt sick, afraid of dying, out of control. She burst to the surface, clawing wildly at the water.

Her feet couldn't touch bottom. She flung her arms desperately, fighting hysteria. Then something pulled her back down, under the surface, and her mind screamed even as she held onto the gulp of air she'd gotten in that second above the water, and for a sickening moment, she didn't know what had gotten hold of her.

All she knew was that she was going to drown because whatever had her, it was pulling her down, deeper, and she couldn't stop it.

Something hit her feet, and she realized with a shock that it was sand. It was the bottom of the lagoon. She contorted her body, fighting frantically, and something pulled her tighter, held down her flailing arms. She was slammed against a hard wall.

No, a chest. A very powerful chest. *Him.* The man who'd called her Tabitha then shoved her into the water even as he claimed he was saving her life. And there was no way she was going to break free of his grip.

She lifted her head, stopped fighting, knew she was going to die now because she couldn't hold her breath one more second, and her eyes locked with a fierce liquid gaze that stunned her, it was so near, and then it was even nearer. Something touched her lips—

His lips.

And in complete, unthinkable shock, she opened her mouth—that was it, she was going to drown—and his mouth closed over hers and suddenly…she was breathing.

She was breathing.

She forgot the water that had been suffocating her a second before. Forgot the deadly men on the bridge, the attacker at the apartment. Forgot that she'd almost been killed more than once in the past twenty minutes.

How could she be breathing?

Then she realized his strong arms had slid around her back and he was stroking her, comforting her, calming her down with efficient control. The sudden gentleness of his hold struck her, and the shocking intimacy of his mouth breathing life into her mouth had her gasp against him, and her tongue touched something warm and sweet. His tongue swept inside her mouth even as he continued to stroke her back, her arms, her shoulders, and she clung, desperate for his air, his amazing, mysterious safety.

Safety that made no sense. She'd been running from him moments before! And yet—he was everything she knew in this dark, wet world, everything keeping her alive. All the pain and fear and panic receded into a surreal vortex as he sweetly and tenderly claimed the last shred of her sanity.

Maybe she was delirious. It was all she could think of. In reality, she was drowning. This couldn't be happening. Her arms were clinging to him, absorbing his unbelievable warmth, her body pressed up against him. She was—oh, God—she was kissing him back and it was like nothing else existed except this hard, wet man holding her at the bottom of the lagoon.

And that realization shocked her so, she jerked back, and the look in his eyes through the dark water made her realize that he was as shocked as she by what had just happened. She held the last breath he'd given her, her heart clanging furiously in her chest, fear returning full force.

He reached up, touched his warm finger to her mouth, and cocked his head, as if listening. Listening to what? All she could hear was the blood pounding in her ears.

Then he placed his mouth on hers again, gently pushing her to open her lips. Oh, God. She did. And her stomach left her body for one more tingling mindless beat. He breathed another breath into her and let go.

A strange energy hummed from him, or maybe it was her. She didn't know anymore.

How could this be happening?

When he pulled away this time, he gave her a long look, nodded as if assuring her of something, grabbed her arm and together they shot upward through the water. Then she was on the surface, and he was pulling her up, onto a bank crowded with weeds and sand. She coughed and fell limp on the dark shore near the bridge.

She lay there, gasping in the air, heavy rain pummeling her—as if she could get any wetter. Then she turned her head and saw him standing over her. Sharply aware of him, she stared up, watching the droplets slide down his cheeks and cascade off his soaked hair and shoulders, the sky darkly wild above him.

His lips were hard, unsmiling, his jaw uncompromising. She felt odd inside, loose and hollow, and he looked utterly, fearsomely, in control. He looked like a tough, dangerous action movie star who was as deadly as his weapons. And yet she wasn't afraid of him now.

Or, at least, not *as* afraid.

He'd just saved her life. For the second time.

"They're gone," he said. "We were down there long enough that they'll think we either ran away or drowned. Either way, we need to get out of here."

The gunmen. The gunmen were gone. Good

thing, since if they were still here, they'd have to kill her where she lay because she felt like one big piece of overcooked spaghetti.

"Who are you?" she breathed. "*What* are you?"

And then she was *sure* she must be delirious because for a second she thought he was going to say something like, *I'm your worst nightmare.* Only maybe that wasn't true. Under the lagoon, he'd been downright fantasy-like, and the memory brought a renewed, inappropriate prickling of sensual heat, and more confusion.

They couldn't have been underwater that long. He couldn't have been breathing air into her lungs. *That wasn't possible.*

She gathered her wits, jerked her loose-limbed, disobedient body into gear and pushed to her elbows. The adrenaline started flowing again.

"Who are *you?*" he grated in return, and he moved swiftly, took hold of her elbow and lifted her to her shaking feet.

For once, he was listening. He was giving her a chance. She grabbed it, desperate.

"Sienna Parker. I'm Sabrina's sister. That was Sabrina's apartment. She's on sabbatical from the university. We both work there. Sabrina—" She stopped. How much did she really want to tell this stranger?

She knew nothing about him. He wanted to

take Sabrina somewhere with him, and he'd been prepared to take her against her will.

"Are you some kind of….police, or—" *How much trouble was Sabrina in?*

"Sabrina's sister," he repeated, ignoring her question, watching her, those steely liquid blue eyes of his searing her to the bone. He reached up with one hand and his warm, wet finger slid across her cheek. Something crackled inside her. He dropped his touch abruptly. "Twin sister?"

She nodded.

"Where is Sabrina?" he demanded.

"I don't know."

"Where is she?"

"I said I don't know! I don't know what's going on. But if she's in trouble, I want to know."

"Oh, she's in trouble," he said.

His eyes on hers were so bright, so sharp, they almost hurt.

"You're scaring me again!" Dammit, what had made her admit that?

"Good."

He was making her angry, too.

"Let's go," he said. "My car."

It didn't sound like an invitation. It was an order.

And dammit, she followed. What other choice did she have? Walk back to Key Mango, hope she didn't run into any gun-toting lunatics along the way?

That option wasn't exactly viable.

The van was gone. Sienna scrambled into the passenger side of the stranger's sedan. He slammed into the driver's seat. Inside the car, the muted sounds of rain and wind tapped and blew. They were both soaked to the skin and she shivered despite the warmth of the island summer night. Shock.

She was in some kind of shock. She was shaking all over.

"You're bleeding," he said. "Your forehead's cut. I'll pick up a first-aid kit somewhere or that'll get infected."

She hadn't even realized. She touched her head, pulled her fingertips away gleaming red in the dim light from the glowing dashboard inside the car. He started the engine and headed the car back toward town.

Her head reeled just a little. What had happened here? She'd gone to Sabrina's apartment, been attacked, chased, run off a bridge, nearly drowned—twice. Now she had willingly gotten into this stranger's car for lack of any better alternative.

This day was so not going well. Her head began to throb and she couldn't stop shaking.

"Why is Sabrina in danger? What did those men want?" What did *he* want? "Who are you?" She couldn't tell a lot about him in this light, but his hair was dark, clipped short, his eyes a fearsome blue. His shoulders seemed to fill the car and he scared her to death at the same time as he made her feel oddly safe.

"My name is Cade Brock," he answered finally.

She hugged her arms around her waist. "So are you the police or what?" Cade Brock. The name buzzed at the back of her mind. Think! She had to think.

Her brain felt as if it had balls bouncing around inside of it.

"Not exactly." He negotiated the dark, wet road like a professional driver.

"What are you exactly, then?" And where were they going? "Is there a police station in Key Mango?"

"We're not stopping in Key Mango."

She cut her eyes to his face again, a nervous twist in her stomach.

Cade Brock. A small gasp escaped her. It all hit her at once. "I know who you are," she breathed harshly, adrenaline rushing her again.

Oh, God. She'd found a magazine in Sabrina's apartment, folded over to an article about treasure hunters. There'd been a photograph of Cade Brock. He was a treasure hunter—a renegade treasure hunter, and some of the quotes in the article had suggested without outright accusation that he was the sort who lived outside the law, sabotaging, scheming and pirating his way into a fortune.

Her head reeled again. Sabrina had said she was afraid of someone, a man. Was it Cade Brock? He was looking for Sabrina. He'd thought she *was* Sabrina. He might have thought her name was Tabitha, but he'd certainly recognized her.

She moved to grip the door handle. The idea of rolling out of the car at this speed, possibly to her death, wasn't appealing.

"Don't even think about it," he said.

Did he read minds, too?

"What do you want with my sister?"

"I want to help her."

"I don't believe you."

"Then that makes two of us, because I'm not sure I believe much you've said so far either. But I saved your life, so that's one point for me, don't you think? And I plan to save Sabrina's life, too. But first I have to stop her."

"Stop her from what?"

"Have you ever heard of the wreck of the *Santa Josefa?* Ramiro's globe?"

Oh, God. She felt hot and cold at once, sick.

Hurting. She didn't want to even think about the *Santa Josefa* and what the search for that shipwreck had done to her family. Ramiro's globe was the legendary artifact discovered by Spanish explorers in the 1700s and, according to survivor reports, carried aboard the doomed *Santa Josefa* as the ship headed back to Spain. Shaped like a globe held up by an outstretched hand, the stone artifact would prove early man once knew the world was round and point to the possibility of ancient interstellar visitors who, legend had it, created it and mapped on its surface the original configuration of earth's tectonic plates. Shipwreck explorers had been looking for the *Santa Josefa* for years.

"Our father used to search for treasure. It was his life." It was his death, too. "Sabrina had all of his old charts and readings. But I don't understand—"

"Did your father find the *Santa Josefa?*" Cade demanded suddenly.

She swallowed hard. "I think so."

For a second, she could almost believe all the air had been sucked out of the car by the intensity of the gaze he burned on her.

"What do you mean you think so?"

"I don't know! We did find something that day. I think it was the globe. But we never brought it up, and then—"

The car seemed to close in on her. Bone-deep grief contracted her chest. *Deep blue water, strobe light dancing through the gloom, fan grass swaying through coral. The globe in her hands. Then the blood—* Pain streaked through her temples.

"What does it matter? We were diving for it that summer. Looking for it. My father was sure we'd found the *Santa Josefa,* that's all I know."

"You said you couldn't swim—"

"I can't swim! Not anymore."

"Can't swim or won't swim?" His expression turned hard, his eyes slicing her.

Was there a difference? She'd have drowned back in that lagoon but for him. Immediate hysteria, that was her reaction to water now.

"What is this about?" she demanded.

The wet, dark night kept spinning past the car windows. Inside, in the glow of the dash, the man beside her, the very strange and frightening man beside her, suddenly looked more like some kind of warrior than a rich playboy.

"Your sister was looking for someone to help finance an expedition to find the *Santa Josefa.* And short of that, she was looking for someone to buy the charts, buy the information. And she was dealing with some very dangerous people."

Sienna sucked in a painful breath. This was so much worse than she'd imagined. "I want to go back to Raleigh," she said. "I want you to take me to the airport. Or take me to a bus station or a police station. I don't care what. I want to go home."

She didn't know how to get in touch with Sabrina now. The last cell phone number she'd had for her sister had been out of service for a week, and her own was at the bottom of the lagoon. She'd left it in the car. But she couldn't stay in Key Mango. Maybe if she went home, Sabrina would call her there.

"You can't go home," he pointed out. "They have your overnight bag, don't they? Did you have some identification in there?"

She nodded mutely.

"And some papers I found in Sabrina's apartment in Raleigh. Our father's charts, with all the sites he'd searched that last summer." She'd found them and brought them with her, intending to confront Sabrina and try to shake some sense into her. "So if that's what they wanted—"

"They want Sabrina," he cut in. "She claimed she knew which site on the chart was the *Santa Josefa*."

"She doesn't know! She wasn't with us that day!"

His look hardened even further. "They don't know that. And they're going to want you now, too. They think her name is Tabitha Donovan, but

they'll use your identification to track you back to
North Carolina. They'll figure out that her real
name is Sabrina Parker, and they'll figure out
you're her sister."

Her life was over. He was telling her that her life
was over. If she went back to Raleigh now, she'd be
hunted down by thugs who wanted to get their hands
on that information. And the ironic thing was, she'd
looked at those charts and she still had no idea which
one had been the *Santa Josefa.* That was fifteen
years ago. It might as well have happened to someone else. She'd woken up that day in the hospital and
they'd had to tell her what had happened to her father. The slices of horrific memory had come later,
but never the whole summer, only bits and pieces.

And she'd never wanted that summer to come
back. She'd never wanted to remember.

"Who are these people?" she asked. "Treasure
hunters?"

"Foreign terrorists."

He might as well have said they were flying
pigs. "What?"

"They're people who blow up buildings and
trains and kill people like you and I breathe. They
think they can use Ramiro's globe to pinpoint hidden weaknesses in the earth's tectonic plates and
set off strategically placed bombs to wipe out the
eastern seaboard."

"That's crazy!" The sick feeling clawed her middle now.

His laser gaze pinned her in the night. "That's not the point now, is it? The fact is, you have two choices right now. You can go back to Raleigh and put yourself in their hands, or you can stick with me and stop your sister before she ruins not just her life, but maybe a whole lot of other lives as well."

He drew to a stop at the one light on the main strip of Key Mango. The businesses were dark, closed, except for a restaurant and a gas station.

Was he really giving her a choice?

What if she got out right now and walked into that gas station and asked for help? Terrorists. If she believed that. And right now she didn't know what to believe.

"I'll go to the police. Or the FBI or the CIA or somebody! Surely they can provide protection. Who do you think you are anyway?" she demanded. He was Cade Brock, playboy and treasure hunter, but that didn't explain everything she'd seen tonight. It didn't explain the way he'd jumped from that car at Sabrina's apartment to shoot it out with those gunmen to rescue her, nor did it explain what had happened in that lagoon, unless she'd imagined that part. And surely she had.

The light changed. He had one eye trained on

the mirror, watching the road behind as they headed for the bridge connecting Key Mango to the
next key.

"You go to the police," he said, "and your sister's going to end up in prison for the rest of her
life. It doesn't matter whether Ramiro's globe can
really provide the sort of information they think
it can—if she helps a terror group find it, she could
end up charged with conspiracy, or worse. You
stick with me, and maybe that won't happen. I
don't want to hurt Sabrina. I want to help her.
She's into something bad, and she's in it over her
head. Whatever game she was playing with these
people, they're tired of it. They weren't playing tonight."

"Why do you want to help her?" And why had
he thought her name was Tabitha? Why would
her sister have been using a false identity? *Because she was up to her eyeballs in something il-
legal.*

Oh, God, he could be telling her the truth. She
didn't want Sabrina to end up in prison. And she
didn't want to end up dead. He'd saved her life
twice tonight. Maybe he could save Sabrina's and
get her out of this mess before she ended up in jail.

"Are you a friend of hers?" she demanded.

"Something like that."

Something like that. That wasn't a real answer.

"What do you want with me?" Maybe—
maybe—he was Sabrina's friend, maybe he wasn't
the man Sabrina had been involved with, but why
would he help her, too? "That was fifteen years
ago. I don't know which one of those sites could
have been the *Santa Josefa.*"

"Did you look at those charts again?"

"Yes. I looked at them. They were my father's original charts. There were ten sites
marked."

"Then you can duplicate them," he said. "That's
a start."

"So what if I help you find the globe? What
then?"

"I'll turn it over to the proper authorities."

Would he? According to what the article had
said, he was rumored to live outside the law when
it came to treasure hunting. And he couldn't know
it, but he might as well have just asked her to poke
a stick in her eye. The last place she wanted to go
was back in time to the shipwreck that had stolen
her father's life, broken her mother's mental health
and nearly destroyed her.

But he was telling her it might be the only way
she could save Sabrina's life and keep her out of
jail. He was right, she had to pick who she would
trust, and she had to pick now. He'd saved her life
twice. That had to mean something.

And if it didn't, then she was about to make a big mistake.

"Shouldn't government authorities already be involved?" she asked, thinking desperately. "If you know—"

"I know because Tabitha—Sabrina—told me. She wanted to know if I'd pay more for the information to find the globe than they were offering. But you're right. Authorities will find out, if they haven't already. Word gets around in the treasure hunting community. That's why there's no time. If we're going to stop this thing, we have to do it now. They've got the charts, but they don't have Sabrina, at least not yet. And I have you."

She didn't want to believe Sabrina would really do this, but he had a point. If they brought up the globe, that would be the end of it. No way could she do it on her own. But Cade Brock…

He would have all the means at his disposal. She swallowed the huge lump in her throat. Did she even care what he did with the globe? All she cared about was Sabrina.

"If I help you find the globe, are you going to help me find Sabrina?"

He cut his hard, blue-black gaze on her. "Oh, we'll find her. I promise you that."

Chapter 4

He'd lied to her. He'd flat-out lied. And the fact that Cade didn't have a choice didn't make him feel any better. He needed Sienna Parker's cooperation and if she knew *he* was the one who could put her sister behind bars, she'd never have agreed to help him.

Undercover work was one lie after another and usually it didn't bother him. This lie did, and he didn't want to think about why—or that it could have anything to do with what had happened in the lagoon.

They hit the turnoff to the Overseas Highway,

but that didn't equal home safe. There was one way, and one way only, to traverse the chain of keys between here and the small airport in Marathon, where a chopper would take them to his island compound on Little Eden. Once there, he'd figure out how to handle Sienna Parker.

And if Chaba's men had decided to double-check the mess they'd left behind back at that bridge near the Key Mango Bird Sanctuary and discovered his car was gone, they'd be looking for it. He didn't want to meet them on U.S. 1, at night, in a storm, with the only lead he had to Chaba, "Tabitha" and the secrets of the *Santa Josefa* in tow.

He needed to find a place to hole up for a few hours, and he needed a new car. He had to get in touch with Beck again, too. Someone needed to get into that Key Mango apartment and find out if Sabrina had ever been there since she'd leased it, and keep an eye out for her to possibly show up. Had something spooked her?

No telling where Sabrina Parker could be now, or what other fake identities she was traveling under. In the meantime, he had to keep Sienna close, and keep her on his side.

She could have a concussion from that brutal slam she'd taken from her unsuccessful abductor, not to mention the car accident. But risking a trip to the hospital in Marathon wasn't tops on his list of things he wanted to do. It was the first place they'd look if they suspected he and the woman had gotten away. He'd have to keep a close eye on her, rely on the emergency training that was part of every PAX agent's basic instruction. He wasn't taking her in for care unless he had no other choice.

"So do you have a plan?" she asked.

In the storm-shadowed car, he could pick out the defensive arch of her pale brows. She had her chin jutted forward, her dark eyes locked warily on him. Was she having second thoughts already? She hadn't had much choice about getting in his car, but there were going to be miles and hours until he could get her to Little Eden.

"We need to get off the highway." He glanced back at the road, not needing the distraction of steeling himself against the confusion and fear warring in her eyes, the emotion he didn't want to know. Or the way her damp hair tangled wildly around her neck, the memory of how soft she'd felt under the water and a whole host of other entirely inappropriate thoughts.

"You think they'll be looking for us?"

"I know they'll be looking for us. They're not sure we're dead to begin with," he pointed out. "And if they track back to that bridge to check on my car, they'll know we're not."

"I don't get it. You said you're a friend of Sabrina's, but you didn't even know her real name. And you're willing to help her, and me, when it's putting your life in danger."

Suspicion wove through every low word she spoke beneath the slap-slap of the windshield wipers as they sped into the night. Nothing but bridges and water and lonely islands... And a handful of killers. Definitely one beautiful woman who didn't trust him any more than he trusted her.

"There's a motel in Big Pine. We can stop there for the night. I should be able to find some place to pick up some antiseptic and a few other things. We'll switch cars in the morning and we shouldn't have any trouble driving into Marathon then."

"That wasn't answering my question," she said sharply. "Am I just supposed to believe you're some kind of benefactor, helping Sabrina when you barely know her, out of the goodness of your heart?"

"I never claimed to have a good heart."

"Then why—"

"Just because I didn't know her real name doesn't mean we weren't friends. Everyone's someone new in the keys, you ever heard that?"

She stared at him, quiet for a minute. "Where are we going after Big Pine?"

"Little Eden."

"What's that?"

"It's a private island, not technically part of the keys." The sign for Big Pine Key whizzed by. "It's where my boat and all my equipment are."

She absorbed that for a beat. "You *own* an island?"

"Just a small one," he said dryly. The island suited his playboy, billionaire, treasure hunter image, but in truth it was his retreat, his haven away from the world. Taking Sienna Parker there wasn't something that made him happy, but he didn't have a choice.

"Right. Just a small one." She was silent for a second, watching him. "I'm not going in the water. You might as well know that right now. I'm not going in the water."

Sienna bit her lip. Even to her own ears, she suddenly sounded almost hysterical. She hated the panic that swamped her at the thought of diving again. She'd been an expert diver at one time. An expert swimmer.

Now, she couldn't even remember what that was like, who that girl had been.

But she had to get a grip, keep her control. This stranger was so *in* control, she couldn't let herself slip around him. Not like she had back at that bridge. Not again.

"I didn't say you had to go in the water," he said finally.

He slowed to the speed limit as they passed shops and restaurants, windows glowing with life in the pouring rain. Pulling into a convenience store, he parked and gave her a long look.

"Let's go in, get a few things for the night," he said. "How are you feeling?"

Her head hurt and she was scared and maybe a little mad.

"I don't think I have a concussion or anything, if that's what you're worried about. Do you want me to tell you who the president is?"

It was hard to tell if he found her amusing or not. Mostly, she thought, *not.*

Her legs felt rubbery as she pushed out of the car and walked ahead of him into the small store. The fluorescent light hurt her eyes. Her head throbbed and she felt as if she were walking in a dream, or maybe a nightmare. She'd gotten on a plane in Raleigh that morning, leaving her apartment and her normal life behind. Nothing was normal about the way her day was ending.

They were both sopping wet, but the store was nearly empty, nobody around to pay any notice to them. The young cashier sat on a stool behind the counter, watching a sitcom rerun on the small TV on the shelf behind him. He barely spared them a glance before going back to his bag of Doritos and *Everybody Loves Raymond.*

In the glare of the store's ceiling lights, she had her first good look at the man who'd pulled her out of the lagoon. He was larger than life, over six feet tall and strong-shouldered. He wore lean, drenched jeans on powerful legs that strode purposefully down the store aisle on booted feet that had been no hindrance to him in the water. She'd lost her sandals at some point, she couldn't even remember when, and her bare feet padded on the cold tile after him. She was tall, nearly five-eight, but he made her feel diminutive.

Or maybe that was more than height. Every ounce of his lean, muscled, mouthwatering back, delineated in the wet black T-shirt he wore, evoked confidence. If someone bothered them here, he looked as if he could squash them like a bug. And if she thought better of their deal and tried to get away...

He stopped, pivoted to look back at her, the liquid blue fire of his eyes reminding her that he was dangerous as well as safe. His dark hair was still plastered to a face that she could see now was brutally handsome. He was all angles and planes and unreadable eyes.

"You okay?" he asked, his voice rough and low.

"Sure." No, she wasn't okay. She wanted to tell him that was a stupid question, but something in his voice stopped her. She could see his gaze flick to the cut on her forehead then back to her eyes, serious and searching.

He wasn't touching her, but her stomach dipped and she wasn't sure if it was because she felt sick with fear and doubts and her throbbing temples, or if it was something else entirely.

She moved past him and began picking out toothpaste, a toothbrush, forcing herself to focus even as her mind was still bouncing all over the place, trying to make sense of everything that had happened. He did the same, and she noticed he grabbed a Key Deer T-shirt set out for the tourist traffic along with a first-aid kit.

"You'll want a change of clothes," he pointed out. Numbly, she picked up a pair of long shorts and a T-shirt and remembered at the last minute to grab a pair of flip-flops, all the small store had to offer in terms of footwear.

It hit her when they reached the counter that she had no money. No wallet. Nothing. She'd lost everything in that overnight bag they'd left behind at the lagoon.

He was taking her to a motel. That was hitting her, too. She could always tell the cashier she needed help, needed a phone.

And possibly get herself killed and never see her nice, safe little library, or Sabrina, again.

The cashier put down his bag of chips and

started ringing up the sale. She shivered and rubbed her hands up and down her arms, knowing the chill had nothing to do with the temperature or how wet she was and everything to do with how unsure she was about the man upon whom she was suddenly completely dependent.

She didn't do dependent. She was master of her own little world with her library, her books, her perfectly balanced accounts.

That world had just disappeared.

The transaction completed, they returned to the car, dashing through the rain for another few seconds, as if she could get any more wet. He shoved the bag onto the floor of the car and started the engine.

"Are you sure we need to stop at a motel?" she asked. "There doesn't seem to be anyone after us." There was an erratic flow of traffic on the rain-swept street, but no one that seemed particularly interested in them. Still…

What was she saying? Did she want to rush off to this private island of his? She wasn't even sure the decision to throw in her lot with his had been the right one.

The pit of her stomach tingled when he slid her a glance in the shadowed car. He turned into a fast-food drive-through a block past the convenience store.

"You were hit on the head," he said quietly. "You could have a concussion, but a stop at the hospital is dangerous right now. I'll keep a close eye on you tonight, but in case there's a reason you need more skilled medical attention, it makes sense to stay in town till morning. And I can't switch the rental car now. It's too late. No point risking showing up at the airport in this car. They have the plates. All around, waiting out the night is the smartest plan."

Nothing about going to a motel with Cade Brock sounded smart to her. She could feel her heart thumping in her chest and a buzz of something that felt suspiciously like arousal. It was unexpected, but so very real, washing her with memories of that kiss under the lagoon.

The drive-through lane was empty and he pulled straight up to the order window.

"What do you want?"

"I'm not hungry."

That was the truth. Her heart was in her throat. No room for food.

He ordered two of everything, ignoring her response.

"I'll get a room with two beds," he said, watching her steadily as they waited for his order to be filled. "But you shouldn't be alone tonight. Not with a head injury. You'll be perfectly safe with me, you can trust me on that."

He was telling her he wasn't going to attack her body once they got into the motel. Was she supposed to be comforted or insulted? She wasn't unattractive, she knew that. But she wasn't as experienced with men as most people seemed to assume. Sure, she'd had relationships, but they'd been few and far between, and the *far between* part seemed to get bigger between each successive relationship. She had her work, but that wasn't it, though it made a good excuse.

The truth was, she wasn't comfortable around men, especially the part of being around men that involved getting naked. And she'd built a life around avoiding situations that made her feel uncomfortable.

There was nothing comfortable about Cade Brock.

"I'm not trusting you on anything," she said by way of warning, shoring up the defenses she so desperately needed. "Just so you know. This is about Sabrina. If she's in trouble, I want to do whatever it takes to get her out of it, and I want to find her. If anything, I mean anything, makes me think you haven't been honest with me about her situation or what we're after and why, I'll make sure you regret it."

He gave her a long look that made her think he didn't buy her tough act. Then he smiled in the night, the lights from the restaurant glancing off the hard angles of his face.

"You might need that bravado of yours before this is over," he said, low. "Good for you."

The order was delivered and he shoved the bag of food and the drinks at her. Hands full, she shifted to face forward again as he drove out of the restaurant lot. Maybe she'd think straighter if she weren't looking at that chiseled profile or those strong shoulders filling up the space next to her. But she could feel him, that intense energy that seemed to radiate off his body.

The small motel a block off the main strip was painted a cheery white with yellow trim, beaming welcome in the spill of a circle of lamplight outside the main office. Cade pulled around to the back and parked out of sight.

She pushed open her door, not waiting for him to come around and open it. Juggling the drinks and the bag of food, she went ahead of him to the rear door that opened into a hallway. A sign indicated that this led to the motel office. Her legs felt rubbery and shaky. Everything that had happened was getting to her, sinking in.

There were a couple of hard chairs across from the check-in desk and she sat down, resisting the urge to close her eyes and fall asleep right there. The adrenaline was falling away and she was completely wiped out, despite the burn of ongoing stress in her veins.

"Hey. Our room's ready."

The slow, deep voice was her first clue that she actually *had* closed her eyes.

"Oh. Okay. Good." She stood, and felt the stiffness that she knew would only be worse tomorrow.

A few minutes later, Cade had a key card in hand along with their bag of goodies from the convenience store, and she was standing in front of room 25 on the second floor. The place was quiet, but she could hear a few thumps and a bark of laughter down the hall that made her think a family with children was in that room. A woman came out of the next room with an empty ice bucket and passed them wearing a robe.

The woman cast her a curious look when Sienna met her eyes. She gripped the food and drinks, trying not to wonder if it was as painfully obvious to everyone else as it was to her that she was about to walk into a motel room with a total stranger. Cade's arm brushed around her waist as he pushed the card in the slot. He let the casual move linger for a beat, as if they weren't strangers at all, then prodded her to move inside as the door slid open.

Once inside, he flicked on the light switch and

moved away from her side. The heat of his touch left her, but the heightened awareness did not. She put the food and drinks down on the dresser and took stock.

"There's one bed." She felt the thump of her heart. "You said there'd be two."

"They said they were out of doubles." He shrugged. "I'll sleep on the floor if it's a problem for you."

If it was a problem for her? She narrowed her eyes and wondered if he was lying or if she had enough energy to care. Let him sleep on the floor. She gave him a tight smile.

"Then that's fine." She walked past him, ignoring whatever the look on his enigmatic face was at her curt reply.

The room was clean, at least, and the curtained sliding door led out to a narrow balcony. Outside, dark ocean and a thin strip of beach met her gaze. Rain tore through the palm trees that lined the path down to the water, lit by evenly spaced landscape lamps.

She let the curtain drop and turned. Cade had moved to switch on the lamp by the bed. He'd turned on every light in the room.

He'd also taken the first-aid box out of the bag. "Let's take a look at that cut now," he said.

"I'm sure I'm fine."

"We'll see about it anyway."

"You're not a doctor. I can clean it myself and dab on some of the antiseptic lotion." She didn't really want him to touch her. Not again. That was when the tingly awareness started up and made her wonder if she had enough sense not to let herself be attracted to a man who was this mysterious and made her this uncomfortable. And who'd probably lied about two beds not being available.

"You could have a scar if it's not stitched up," he pointed out.

She blinked. "You're not stitching up my head and it's not safe for us to go to the hospital, I'm assuming, so I'll deal."

Turning to the mirror over the cheap dresser, she peered into it, her pulse thunking hard in her veins. He was right. She was definitely going to have a scar, but what was one more? Now that she was taking her first look at herself, she wanted to laugh at the idea that he would even think twice about jumping her bones.

She looked like a drowned rat that had been beaten up first just for fun. How sexy.

Her hair was tangled in a wild mess around her shoulders. There was a purplish bruise that was going to look worse tomorrow starting to bloom along the side of her face where she'd been struck with the gun, and an ugly, inch-long gash just over her left eyebrow where she'd hit her forehead in the accident.

She felt like crying, and maybe if she'd been alone, she would have let herself do that.

But she wasn't alone.

His face appeared above her shoulder in the mirror, dark and somber and concerned in a way that made her feel strange and almost glad he was there. He looked so damn competent, but—

"I wasn't going to suggest I stitch it up," he said. "I'm not a doctor. There are butterfly bandages in the first-aid kit, though."

The harsh lights of the lamps turned on all over the motel room played unforgivingly on the face of the man behind her. He was unbelievably good-looking in a brutal I-could-kill-you-with-my-bare-hands way, but she could see experience etched in those hard angles and planes, and maybe a little pain. What pain would a man like Cade Brock carry?

His eyes held hers in the mirror, only they weren't as hard now. There was a softening, an empathy that suggested he wouldn't think less of her if she did have a minor meltdown right now.

"You have to trust me a little bit sometime, Sienna Parker," he said softly, "or we'll never save your sister. I'm trying to help you here."

She turned, shocked by the nearness of that

searing gaze of his. And maybe a bit surprised, too, by how much she longed to do just that. Trust him. More than little bit, even.

Alarm bells sounded in her veins and she could feel her heart banging against the wall of her chest.

"I'm not sure about that yet," she said flatly.

Chapter 5

If he hadn't already bought his ticket to hell a long time ago, he'd be on his way now. *Of course* there were double rooms available. And the shrewd look in her eyes told him she was betting that was true. But she wasn't calling him on his lie.

She wasn't having anything to do with him if she could help it either, though. She'd showered and changed into the clothes he'd bought her at the Quik Pak in Big Pine and put her own butterfly bandage on by the time she came out of the bathroom. Cade didn't want to give her points for anything, but she'd been pretty tough so far. She was willing to cross the line, risks be damned, for her sister. It touched a sore spot inside him he wanted to forget existed. He didn't want her to be complicated. He didn't want to respect her. He didn't want to *feel* anything for her at all. He needed to use her.

He sat in a chair by the small table in the corner where he'd just finished the meal from the fast-food restaurant. He watched as she walked to the bed, pulled down the gold tone-on-tone motel bedspread and sat.

There were scrapes on her arms, and a bruise growing on her cheek. She had to be hurting. He could see it in the careful way she held herself, the pain shimmering far back in those guarded eyes.

By this time tomorrow—sooner—he'd know a lot more about Sabrina and Sienna Parker. He'd used the privacy while she was in the shower to call PAX headquarters. They'd have a man at that apartment in Key Mango tomorrow to see what he could find, and he had no doubt that background checks on the Parker women had been initiated as soon as he'd clicked off the call.

"Eat something," he said.

She ignored his direction and turned out the light by the bed, leaving the lamp lit on the dresser. For a long moment, she sat there, meeting his gaze across the shadows. She was afraid, and that got to him whether he liked it or not. She could be completely innocent of any conspiracy with her sister. Certainly, she appeared shocked by everything that had happened.

But she was caught up in the middle of it now, and she was scared.

She was scared of *him*. He didn't like that fact, and the proud way she tried to hide it from him only made her seem that much more vulnerable. A tenderness swelled inside him, almost painful. He had no business feeling anything for this woman. She was a pawn in his mission, nothing more.

"I'd feel better if you ate something," he said.

"I'm not trying to make you feel better."

He found himself resisting the urge to laugh. The situation wasn't funny. She needed her strength, more than she knew yet. "How do you feel?"

"I'm okay."

"I'm not going to hurt you, you know."

She held his gaze unflinchingly, chin tipped. "You attacked me, threw me to the ground and pinned me down tonight. So don't give me any bull now. I know what you're capable of if I don't do what you want."

Guilt stabbed him. "I thought you were your sister then."

"Right. My sister. Your friend. I'd hate to see

what you do to your enemies. Oh, wait. I know. You blow their heads off."

"I'm just trying to do the right thing here, whether you understand that or not," he said. She had no idea how true his statement was. Maybe it was the most honest thing he'd said to her so far.

"You're just an honorable man, is that it? A hero." Her voice was tinged with sarcasm.

She couldn't know that her words stung. He was no hero. He fought for a cause, for justice, but it wasn't heroic. He had nothing else to live for, nothing else to fight for. PAX was his life, had been for as long as he could remember. And the chance to nail Chaba… That was the dream of a lifetime.

"I'm after the same thing you are. To stop Sabrina before she makes a big mistake."

"Sabrina is my sister, my family. She's the only family I have left. I love her. Your motives are a lot less clear."

There was a challenge in her cool voice, along with a thread of anxiety she couldn't cloak despite her best efforts. She was desperately worried about her worthless sister.

In the short silence that followed, she curled her legs up onto the bed and reached for the covers. In the beat before she pulled the sheet up, he caught a tantalizing glimpse of skin as the long

shorts she'd bought—and was wearing to bed—
rode up, a glimpse of a long, terrible scar that
fired all the way up her thigh.

His gaze flicked to her face, and he saw something in her eyes tighten as she yanked the sheet,
covering her legs. Whatever it was, whatever had
happened to her, she hadn't wanted him to see
it. In spite of himself, something in his chest
banded.

Did she not know how sexy she was, even in
that huge, shapeless shirt, scar be damned? And
fascinating. He couldn't deny it. He was fascinat-
ed by all those complications that made her too
real to him. Afraid and proud. Vulnerable and
strong.

He would rather have put it all down to her
prettiness, but that would be another lie. Even as
he'd appreciated Sabrina's looks, he hadn't been
attracted to her, not one bit.

And he couldn't afford to be attracted to Sienna.

He gathered his thoughts. "Why wasn't Sabrina
with you that day?"

"She wasn't with us all that summer. She'd
been in trouble."

"What kind of trouble?"

"She was pregnant."

He let that sink in. "What happened?"

Her mouth hardened. She didn't want to answer, he could see that. "My parents sent her to stay with an aunt. She stayed there till she had the baby. It was put up for adoption. She was there at the hospital when I woke up. She didn't want to talk about it then, and so much else had happened—"

"What exactly happened that day? What happened to your father?"

The tight look on her face almost hurt him to watch. "He was attacked by a shark," she said briefly.

His gut sank. That was what had happened to her leg. She'd been attacked, too. She'd lived, but her father had died. And she'd watched him die.

Can't swim or won't swim?

Now he was betting he knew the answer, along with some good guesses about a few other things. She'd survived, but that wouldn't have been without an emotional price he knew all too well.

"How did you know where to find Sabrina in Key Mango?" he asked, veering the conversation away from a subject that made him feel far too connected with a woman who was a pawn. "How did you know about the apartment?"

She arranged the thin motel pillows behind her head before she answered him. Watching her, he felt a tightening of heat in his groin, that attraction that had no place in this mission. He couldn't do anything about the fact that he was a man, with very human physical responses despite his mutations. But he shouldn't, and wouldn't, act on those responses.

But if that were true, why had he kissed her in the lagoon? Unbidden came the memory of that kiss, and her response to him.

He needed to keep his distance from her, to the extent that it was possible. But he needed answers, too, and as much as he wanted to get out of the damp clothes sticking to his body—and he wouldn't shower and change until she was asleep— there were still too many questions clamoring at his mind. Something was wrong with what had happened at that apartment. He just didn't know what.

"She sent me a letter," Sienna finally answered. "She asked me to come down and she gave me a copy of the apartment key. I'd talked to her on the phone not too long before that and she'd been talking about a man, a man who scared her."

"Did she give you a name?"

She shook her head. "She promised me she wasn't going to have anything more to do with him. She wanted me to come down and we'd have a good time."

"Did she ask you to bring those charts that were in your bag?" he asked then.

"No. I have a key to her Raleigh apartment and I found them there. I was worried about her because her cell phone was disconnected, but she'd told me to come, so I came—and really, by then, I was worried enough that I would have come even if she hadn't sent me the key to the Key Mango place. Anyhow, I was checking on her apartment and I found the charts. We both work at the same university—me in the library and Sabrina in the marine archaeology department."

"Why did you bring the charts here?"

"I was going to confront her with them. I didn't even know she had them till I found them there. I hadn't seen those charts in fifteen years. I was afraid—" Her forehead knit and she bit her lip.

"Afraid of what?"

"I was afraid she was going after the *Santa Josefa*. I knew she was down here diving. After our father died, Sabrina didn't want to stop diving. We did stop, for years, both of us. Our mother—" She stopped, and he waited through the pause. The rush of the wind outside filled the still motel room. "In college, once she was out on her own, Sabrina started diving again, on school holidays and summers, just with friends, nothing that was a big deal. But when she took the sabbatical, I knew it was different. She was going to start treasure hunting again." She pushed down on the bed, sliding further under the covers. "I'm tired. I'm going to sleep."

She flipped around, showing him her back.

"You didn't like that. You didn't want her to dive again."

She sighed, annoyed with him or her sister, or possibly both of them, and flipped back.

"Yes, of course. I was worried about it. It can be dangerous and— I was worried she was going to get addicted, the way our father was, all right? I was worried she'd never come back from the sabbatical. And when I found the *Santa Josefa* papers, I knew it was true. I don't know what you're getting at."

Something hard and strong thrummed in his veins. His gut tightened and he felt a sudden urge to put his hands around Sabrina Parker's neck and shake her. The burst of protective ferocity for Sienna stunned him, and he worked to shove it aside, concentrate on the here and now and the woman before him.

"When you got to the apartment in Key Mango," he pointed out, "she wasn't there waiting for you. Why do you think that was?"

He knew why, suddenly he knew why. And he was sure of it. It made too much sense not to be true.

"Maybe she knew someone would—"

"Maybe she set you up."

"No!" the word exploded out of her and she sat straight up in the bed. For a second, he thought she was going to bolt up off the mattress and come over to where he sat. Maybe slap him.

But she sat there, rigid and angry, the sheet sliding down around her.

He made his voice steady, flat, left it to his words alone to convince her of the ugly possibility. "You're identical twins. Maybe she was going to let them take you, let them think they had her. Maybe that was the breathing room she needed."

"Sabrina wouldn't do that to me." Her voice wasn't steady at all.

"Are you sure?"

The spattering of rain against the balcony door as the wind changed sounded as angry as the hot thread tangling through her voice.

"This conversation is over," she bit out.

She flipped around again, dragging the sheet up to her chin, and this time she didn't turn back and he didn't ask her any more questions. He'd planted the seed of doubt, whether she was ready to face it or not.

Eventually, if they found the globe, and if they found Sabrina, the truth would hit her in the face. And he didn't like the fact that he cared that Sienna would be immeasurably hurt.

* * *

Sleep. She needed to sleep, for about two hundred hours. She was exhausted, but the rough, dangerous man she knew was sitting in that chair across the room from her kept her awake.

Maybe she set you up.

It was a heinous thing to say, a heinous thing to even suggest, and he'd sounded like he was more than suggesting it. He'd sounded like he was sure. There was no way he could be right, but then why was she so unsettled and anxious that she couldn't sleep?

Why would she even think of believing anything he said? He was a stranger and Sabrina was her sister.

Could you call a man you'd kissed a stranger?

She didn't want to think about that, either. Even now, her stomach dipped and she felt hot inside when she thought about those stunning moments in the lagoon. Well, it could only have been one moment, surely. They couldn't have been under the water for that long.

The memory of that kiss, the strangeness of thinking he was breathing air into her lungs... It all seemed so bizarre now. Clearly she hadn't been thinking straight all evening, and that explained why she'd let doubt creep into her heart.

She determinedly squeezed her eyes shut and

forced her mind to focus on relaxing her aching body.

Who was Cade Brock, really? Was he more than a playboy treasure hunter with nothing better to do than rescue Sabrina, a person he barely knew? The only thing she could count on for a fact was that Sabrina was in some kind of trouble, and even if it meant she was stepping into the trouble after her, the one hope in hell she had of finding her sister and uncovering the mess—and fixing it—was to stick with Cade.

Even if he likely was part of the mess.

Maybe she'd wake up tomorrow and find the whole thing had been a nightmare. Nothing about tonight seemed real, especially the part where she was stuck in a motel room with a mysterious stranger and armed gunmen on the loose who wanted to kidnap her or worse.

And Cade… If she knew for sure what *he* wanted, maybe she'd be able to sleep.

She lay very still, keeping her breathing steady, and after a long, long time she heard him get up from the chair. She heard the bag rustle and knew he was getting his things. The soft whisper of his footsteps moved across the carpeted floor, and the bathroom door slid quietly shut. She heard the water come on.

He'd waited until he thought she was asleep before showering. Was he afraid she'd take off? He had to be.

She toyed with the idea of doing just that for exactly fifteen seconds. Where would she go? What would she do? What better chance did she have of finding Sabrina, and keeping herself alive, than with Cade Brock?

As dangerous as he might be, he was also her only tie to Sabrina's secret world. And despite the kiss, she didn't know the first thing about the man on whom she was staking Sabrina's life, and maybe her own. Was he even who he said he was? He claimed to be Cade Brock, and she'd accepted it because she'd read his name and seen his picture in a magazine. Maybe he just bore a passing resemblance to Cade Brock. It wasn't as if she'd studied that article.

Everybody is someone new in the keys.

He had to take off his pants, put down his identification, to step into the shower. She'd seen him whip open his wallet in the store and in the fast-food drive-through. There was identification in there. It could be fake, of course, but it was all she had to go on.

Sitting up on the bed, she silently slid back the sheet and tiptoed across the floor. Adrenaline rushed through her again. The handle to the bathroom door turned in her grip. It wasn't locked!

Damp heat folded over her as she stepped into the bathroom. The curtain was pulled tight across the combination shower and tub. A pile of clothes lay on the floor, and on the counter sat the bag of essentials from the convenience store. A toothbrush and shaving kit spilled out, and beside the bag lay a leather wallet.

And a gun.

Her pulse tripped at the sight of the weapon. She'd known he had a gun, of course, but had forgotten. She hadn't seen him with it in his hand since the incident at the apartment. Either he'd had it hidden on his person, or maybe he'd had it tucked away somewhere in the car and brought it in without her noticing....

It looked heavy and deadly and it made her realize all over again that she was scared of this man. The last time she'd seen a gun up close, it had been her father's. He'd kept a rifle and speargun on his boat to fend off sharks and unethical treasure hunters who would occasionally attempt to steal a discovery.

He hadn't had a gun in his hand the day a shark had bitten him in two.

Cade Brock, if that was his real name, was a renegade treasure hunter himself. And he certainly seemed well accustomed to carrying a gun.

Hurry. She jerked herself out of the shock of seeing the gun and reached for the wallet beside it, flipped the leather fold over to the Florida driver's license.

Cade Brock. The address was an apartment in Miami, though it sounded as if he lived on Little Eden. Of course, he was rich. He probably had homes all over the place—

The water stopped running and the curtain rod holders scraped back, shooting her heart into her throat.

She spun, and her breath caught. He stood there, superhero action man, magnificently naked, aqua-blue eyes pinning her. For a stunning beat, all she could do was stand there, locked in place by those overpowering, dangerous eyes, her natural protective instinct to run left unheeded. Her heart was pounding so hard, she thought she'd faint.

"What do you want?" he demanded.

Oh, God. For just a second, what she wanted and what was smart went in completely divergent directions.

"I want to know the truth about you," she said, her voice shaking.

His gaze narrowed, darkened, and then he moved. Every naked, powerful inch of him moved toward her.

The gun must have leaped off the bathroom counter by itself, because she had no idea what she was thinking when she picked it up.

Chapter 6

He grabbed her wrists, slamming her hard against the bathroom counter. The gun clattered against the side of the toilet then thunked to the tile floor. In the space of a second Cade had her pinned and helpless, his naked thighs straddling her, crushing her against the counter ledge with his weight.

For a moment she was silent, then she opened her mouth. Before she could scream and wake everyone up, he released one of her hands to clamp his over her mouth, twisting her around so that he held her with his other arm.

Impressions struck him of her very round bottom soft against his hardness and the fear in her searing brown eyes, before all he could sense was her wild hair, its sweet scent filling his nostrils. Then she was fighting again, bucking against him.

He held her fast. "Stop it," he growled, "and I'll let you go."

She twisted her head, one eye locking with his, angry and desperate.

"Don't scream," he warned.

He could feel her chest heave, but she nodded, stopped fighting. He let her go, and dammit she turned right around, kicked him in the naked groin and in a blur ran from the bathroom. He swore and raced after her. Catching her at the motel room door, he spun her around and pinned her arms over her head.

Ragged breaths tore out of him. "You are a freaking workout, Sienna Parker." He caught his breath.

Her eyes raged at him. "Let me go."

He held her even tighter, her slender wrists nothing against the force of his hands pinning them to the door. Then he saw the tears glistening in her eyes, and something hard stabbed him in the chest.

Guilt.

Dammit, he was hurting her, scaring her. He

didn't want to do that. He needed her trust, and then it hit him that he not only needed her trust, he actually wanted it. He wanted that scared look out of her eyes. And this was no way to accomplish it.

He'd already made several stupid mistakes. He'd let her fake him out that she was asleep and he hadn't locked the bathroom door, then he'd let her nail him in the balls. Sienna Parker was throwing his radar off, big time, and he had to stop it.

"What the hell do you think you're doing?" he demanded, rough despite his intention to be cool. "Why were you sneaking into the bathroom after me?"

"I want to know who you are," she gasped. "I want to know if your name is really Cade Brock. I want to know what you want with my sister!"

"I think we've been over that."

"I think I don't believe you! How do I know you're who you say you are? How do I know whether to believe anything you say?"

"Trust me."

"Go to hell!"

Time locked for a strange moment, and he felt the electric pull of her proud eyes with that wisp of vulnerability hidden deep inside. Touching him. And he didn't let anything touch him. Not ever.

"I thought we had a plan," he said, not letting

go even as she struggled, her curvy body straining against him.

"*You* have a plan. Now if you're done proving that you're stronger than me, get your hands off me."

"First I want to know if you're going to go tearing out of here like a bat out of hell and screaming the motel down."

Her lips clamped together tightly before she opened them to speak.

"I want to know things, too. I want to know just who you are. I want to know how you met my sister. I want to know what the hell you want and why you're involved. And I want the truth this time."

Wary eyes fired at him. Outside, the rain had stopped, and the motel lay suddenly silent around them.

"I told you my name." And that was the truth— Cade Brock was his real name. He considered what else he should tell her, the best way to play the information. "I met your sister with some diving acquaintances. She told me she was looking for someone to bankroll a search for the *Santa Josefa*. She told me about the charts. She offered to sell them to me. I met her in a bar in Key West. I walked her outside and a man named Harmon Kerbasi cut my throat." He watched her eyes flare. His gut tightened. "Kerbasi works for a man named Adal Chaba. He's a terrorist thug who'd been hiding out from the U.S. government for twenty-five years, ever since he blew up an entire village to try to retake control of a Pacific island he'd turned into a virtual slave camp. She's in trouble. She's been dealing with some really bad people."

"When was this?"

"About a month ago."

She blinked, and he could see her gaze drop to his neck, see as she took in the still-red and narrow slice of a scar.

"I talked to her a few weeks ago," Sienna said, but her voice was thin, trembly, even as she tipped her chin. "She didn't say anything about being in danger other than some man who frightened her. I got the impression it was someone she was involved with, in a relationship. Maybe it was you, for all I know. She asked me to come see her in Key Mango. You said you thought she set me up. Do you think she set you up?"

"I think she told Kerbasi I was interested in the globe. I think she was playing both ends against the middle. She made a phone call in the bar before we walked outside. I think that she decided I hadn't offered her enough money, and that she knew Kerbasi wanted me out of the way. I was competition for the globe. And I'm betting they paid her for that little setup. Your sister likes money, Sienna." He couldn't tell her about the Swiss bank account or the phone call PAX had intercepted between Kerbasi and "Tabitha" that proved she'd set him up.

"That's a lot of *you think* this and *you think* that," Sienna shot back. "And if you really think all of that, why would you try to help her now?"

Damn her persistence. "I want the globe," he said. "I want it for myself. If I have it, she can't sell it to the terrorists. She'll be out of trouble, that's all that should matter to you."

"You said you'd turn it over to the authorities!"

"I lied. I want it for my private collection."

"And you think I should trust you!"

"Can you trust *them* more? What do you care what I do with it as long as your sister doesn't end up in prison?"

She had a choice, him or them. And if he'd just made himself only slightly less of a son of a bitch than the men back at the bridge, he'd have to live with it. He'd have to live with the wrenching disgust in her eyes, too.

"I knew you were lying," she spat at him. "You make me sick. And I don't believe you about Sabrina setting you up, or me. She couldn't have known. She's in this, whatever this is, over her head."

That, at least, was one truth between them. He wanted to damn her for being too smart, too persistent, to buy his line that he wanted to help Sabrina because he was her friend. He just hadn't expected the price, but he'd get over it.

Or so he had to believe. He didn't get close to people, not ever, and on a job, it was the last mistake he could let himself make. Sienna was an innocent, he was more sure of that with every minute he spent with her, and he wasn't used to dealing with innocent people, that's all. He'd let her proud, scared eyes get to him.

He didn't care, and couldn't care, what she thought about him. He just needed her cooperation. The mission, nailing Chaba, was first and foremost. That was all he needed, all he cared about.

"I've answered your questions," he said. "Now you answer mine."

Her eyes darkened and her jaw set.

"I'll help you find the *Santa Josefa,* for Sabrina's sake. And then I hope you rot in hell."

His mouth curved up in a smile that felt harsh.

"I'm sure you'll get your wish." He let go of her hands and stepped back. "I'm going to get dressed and you're going to get back in that bed and get some sleep."

She kept her eyes on his face, not glancing down, and for a second, he almost wanted to laugh at the discomfit in her expression as if she'd suddenly remembered that he'd been holding her captive, a breath between them, while he stood there buck naked.

And then he saw something else glance across her eyes, something like hurt, or even disappointment. Whatever it was, it made him feel like that much more of a bastard. If she'd had the mistaken impression that he was some kind of hero, it was for the best she'd figured out her error now. He didn't care what she thought of him.

She whipped past and left him standing there alone in his lies.

Sienna was shaking as she pulled the covers back up over her body. She should have stayed put to begin with, then she could have fooled herself into believing that he was with some kind of macho hunk who rescued women as a hobby. But as soon as the thought crossed her mind, she knew it wasn't true.

She wanted, needed, to know the truth about Cade Brock. Even if she didn't like it.

She'd gotten him naked, in more ways than one. She knew the dark motivation of his determination to find the globe. Saving Sabrina was a side benefit, not the goal for him. And she was just a tool. She had to remember that, too.

Other things she wished she could forget, like how he'd looked when he stepped out of that shower, all chiseled muscles of corrugated iron. Oh, she'd known he was strong, that had been obvious with his clothes on. With them off, she'd been stunned by the awesome, almost savage definition of his body.

Brawny and virile, yet without the bulk of a weight lifter. His sinewy muscles looked like they'd been formed from real work. No doubt he was an expert diver and used to dealing with a lot of heavy equipment, but even so, she'd been surprised by just how powerful he looked, not to mention shocked by that vicious scar he'd blamed on Sabrina.

She'd also been shocked by her reaction to his body. Her heart had zinged into her throat and her nerve endings had positively tingled. When he'd asked her what she wanted, something hot and all wrong inside her body had answered him and it had made no sense. He was mouthwateringly built, that was a given, but he was also dangerous and secretive and a criminal. She'd seen him kill a man in Key Mango as if he were flicking a flea off his arm. He was human, that scar proved he wasn't invulnerable, but he was also fundamentally different from any man she'd ever met.

Even average guys tended to make her nervous, tongue-tied, awkward. But she wasn't tongue-tied with Cade. She'd held a gun on him, then told him to go to hell.

She was more scared of herself, almost, than of him.

What was wrong with her? She couldn't trust him, and she wasn't sure if she could trust herself either.

She heard him come out of the bathroom. She felt his energy move through the room, that tingling awareness she couldn't block no matter how she tried. The light across the room snapped off. The silence now that the storm had passed felt heavy and intimate. Then she felt him sit down....

On the bed.

She whipped around, pushing up onto her elbow. He was right there, in her face, stretching his big, fine form down on the mattress beside her. He hadn't lifted the sheet, just parked himself on top of the covers. There was enough light from the motel patio and walk below slipping in between the crack in the drapes for her to make out the shadowy outline of his body.

"What are you doing?" Shrieking. She was shrieking. She grabbed a desperate, calming breath as he plumped his pillow and ignored her. "I said, what are you doing?"

"Going to bed."

"This is *my* bed!"

"This is the only bed."

"You said you would sleep on the floor."

"I changed my mind."

"I haven't!"

He just kept lying there, a foot away from her on the big bed, lazily watching her. He'd put a shirt on, and a pair of athletic shorts. Even through the thin material of the T-shirt and the shadows, she could see his powerful physique, and when he stretched his arms to position them over his head, the muscles of his upper arms bunched and caught the scant light.

And she was staring.

She jerked her gaze off his body and back to his face. She could just make out the shine of his eyes.

"You lied about a room with two beds, didn't you?" she demanded.

"Maybe," he said, no inflection in his voice revealing if he was annoyed or amused. He was just…toneless. Completely undisturbed by the prospect of sleeping in a bed with her, a stranger. And why that pissed her off instead of comforting her, she couldn't answer, but it did. *She* was not undisturbed.

"I'm tired," he said. "I could use a good night's sleep. It's stupid for one of us to sleep on the floor. I'm not going to jump your bones. I've already told you that."

"You told me a bunch of other lies, too."

"I'm not lying about this. Unless you want me

to be." Now his eyes sparked in the night. "I've never taken a woman against her will in my life, and I'm not going to start now."

She stared at him, frustrated and curious all at once.

"Have you had many women?" Why had she asked that? She wanted to take back the question instantly, but it was impossible. He'd made her feel silly and childish about sharing the bed, and maybe a little…unwanted, which was ridiculous. Did she want to be fending off his advances? Of course not.

The shadowed line of his hard mouth twitched, almost a smile but not quite. If it had been a smile, for a brief period of time, it had been an oddly painful one.

"Hundreds," he said.

Then he closed his eyes, as if she weren't even there, as if she were of no consequence whatsoever and he could, *snap,* put her and their situation out of his mind.

She flopped back on her pillow, staring up at the dark ceiling, wishing she could forget him as easily as he appeared to forget her. No way was she dropping into instant, blessed slumber. Not with superhero action man on the bed beside her.

"If you have a girlfriend, I'm sure she wouldn't like you sleeping with another woman."

Cade's voice slid through the shadows. "Sleeping and having sex are not the same thing, Sienna."

"It's not exactly…proper." Oh, God, she'd been a librarian too long.

A guffaw cracked the night and she wanted to hit him, really hit him this time. Maybe right in the balls like she had before.

"Stop thinking."

Stop thinking. "You'd like that, I'm sure." But she had to admit, it would be easier if she didn't think so much.

"Go to sleep, Sienna. Or at least shut up so I can."

She lay there listening to his even breathing, loud suddenly to her overaware ears. Overaware of him and everything about him—his heat, his scent, his physical power over her.

Was he really asleep?

If she got off the bed, she was absolutely sure he would know, absolutely sure that lying down next to her was what he'd intended all along. He'd know if she got up, know if she tried to walk out the door, know if she thought better of sticking with him. He'd probably spring into instant awareness if she so much as moved her pinkie toe.

Was she a hostage? Was this all a game, that he'd convinced her she was going with him to Little Eden voluntarily?

The worst part of the questions that kept her awake was the fact that she didn't think any of the answers mattered. Barring the unlikely miracle that everything that had happened tonight was a dream, she needed him as much as he needed her. Maybe more.

Chapter 7

Cade checked his gun by the morning light peering in through the thin shield of the motel room drapes, then slid it into the ankle holster strapped beneath his right jean leg. His pants had dried enough overnight that he could put them on again despite some lingering dampness. He tried not to look at the woman sleeping a few feet away, her limbs flung out in every direction, sheets twisted and falling away to reveal the long, sweet curve of her body.

He didn't need to look at her. He didn't need to be anywhere near her, but that part couldn't be helped.

She'd been angry last night. He'd been angry, too. More at himself than at her.

He heard her move, stretch and flop over on the bed. He looked. Big mistake. She was on her stomach now, her shirt riding up to bare a breath of her middle, the round cheeks of her buttocks delineated through the shorts she'd picked up at the convenience store, long shorts that he knew now she'd chosen to hide that scar on her thigh. He tried to not remember how those soft cheeks had felt pressed up against his bare body last night in the bathroom.

He'd told her the truth when he said he'd never in his life taken a woman against her will, but what he hadn't told her was that he wanted her, bad. If she hadn't been so scared when he'd pinned her down after he'd caught her going through his things, she'd have noticed the proof of it, too.

There was more than one pressing reason they needed to find Ramiro's globe, and find it fast.

She flopped over onto her back now and opened her eyes.

"Get up," he said, more roughly than he'd intended. "We need to get going."

She blinked blearily, and he could see both himself and the night before coming into focus in her eyes. The side of her face held a blooming blue bruise that made the rest of her features look that much more pale.

"How are you feeling?" he asked, gentler. It wasn't her fault he couldn't keep the mission on his mind when he looked at her. As much as he needed to keep what distance he could between them, he also couldn't forget that she was innocent and vulnerable and he owed her protection, even from himself.

"I'm okay," she said automatically, but he could see the strained grimace of her mouth as she pushed to a sitting position. She was bound to be sore and aching this morning.

And despite the fact that touching her was a bad idea, he found himself striding to the bed and reaching for her arm to help her up.

"I don't need your help." She pushed him away. "Once I get going, I'll be fine." She walked, slowly, to the bathroom and closed the door. He heard the water come on in the sink.

A few minutes later, she came back out. He'd gathered their things and was standing at the door, waiting.

"I'm hungry," she told him. "And I'll need more clothes." She frowned, her forehead knitting, the butterfly bandage crinkling, reminding him of how many ways she'd been hurt. "I keep thinking I should call someone, let them know where I am, but—"

Did she have someone to call? Was there a man

in her life? He bit off the question before he could voice it.

"I took two weeks off work. No one's expecting me. I wish I could talk to Sabrina." Her voice was low, and threaded with an ache that reached in his chest and grabbed at his heart. "I just wish—"

Wishes weren't going to do her any good, and that was a harsh reality she'd have to face.

"Let's go," he said.

She walked toward him, watching him as if he were a particularly unsavory specimen in a petrie dish and if she got too close, she might be contaminated. He was used to that, but the tight ping in his veins told him it was different when she did it.

He cared what she thought of him, dangerous as that was. It was also unfixable. She thought he was lower than dirt and the best thing he could do for himself and for her was to keep it that way.

"Where did this come from?" she asked when they got outside to the parking lot and discovered a different rental car in the spot where they'd left his car the night before.

"I arranged for another car to be delivered first thing this morning," he told her. Truth was, the PAX team who would be checking out the Key Mango apartment had switched out the cars for him on their way. That was just one of many pesky details Sienna Parker didn't need to know. He was lone wolf Cade Brock, renegade treasure hunter. He didn't have a team of agents backing him up, none that Sienna would know about.

And for the most part, he did work alone. He was deep undercover, living his Cade Brock playboy lifestyle, pretending his life away. Luckily, it also involved a lot of time alone on the sea, the only place he felt at home. The only place he felt real.

Other than necessary communications, Cade didn't need contact. Besides, unless PAX turned up something concrete, like the artifact, they had other fish to fry, despite their keen interest in Chaba. Since the discovery of supernatural stones several months ago, the race had been on to uncover more possible connections to South American artifacts of interstellar origin. Having been discovered in the same region by Spanish explorers, Ramiro's globe may or may not be tied into that hunt. PAX wouldn't know till Cade found the globe and got it back to the League for study by Nina Phillips, now Nina Tremaine. She'd been behind the revelation of the El Zarpa stones, the find that had triggered the League's interest in interstellar artifacts.

Sienna Parker sat with her arms crossed, her black-and-blue cheek turned away from him, the rising sun sliding through the car windows drifting an angelic haze around her profile. He pulled into the fast-food drive-through down the road from the motel again.

"You going to eat this time?" he asked her.

"I said I'm hungry."

She smelled good, better than the sausage and bacon biscuits wafting in from the drive-up window. He passed a bill to the cashier and she handed back his change and a bag with a couple of egg croissants and coffees. Sienna popped the lid off her cup and steam swirled up. He ate as he drove one-handed, then slammed down the coffee, trying to stop thinking about the woman next to him, who looked cold even as she cupped the hot cup of coffee in her hands.

"How far to the airport?" she asked, and despite her tipped chin and square gaze, trepidation lurked in the shadows of her amber eyes.

"We're almost there." In fact, the Marathon Airport sign zipped past.

"Exactly where is this island?"

"Little Eden is about forty miles due west off the tip of the keys. It's not connected by the Overseas Highway, and so not considered part of the keys. It's always been privately owned."

"Are you flying us out there? Do you have your own plane, too?"

"I have my own helicopter, yes." There was a

helipad on the island. "I'm a licensed pilot, don't worry."

"I've never been in a helicopter before."

She didn't look excited for this to be a first. Or maybe it was just the company.

"It's a short flight," he told her. "We'll be there before you know it." And then it would be way too late for her to back out, which he still suspected she was considering.

He pulled into the rental car drop-off lot and they walked from there to the terminal building. Major airlines didn't service the small airport, so Sienna would have come in through the larger airport in Key West, and he could see her surprise at the stunningly upgraded multimillion dollar facility with its Spanish tiles, lofty ceilings, and displays of local artistry. They stopped in the airport boutique store where he had her pick up more clothes.

Once finished, and keeping a wary eye as long as they were in the public areas, he placed his palm against the small of her back. She didn't know it, but backing out wasn't even an option.

Sienna squeezed her eyes shut as the helicopter rose into a steep hover, the deafening roar of the spinning rotors filling the surprisingly roomy cabin. As usual, Cade Brock looked stunningly competent as he took the pilot's seat. Was there anything he couldn't do?

She should have woken up this morning and informed him that this whole plan was crazy and called the police. Contacting the authorities was sane. Taking off for the wild blue yonder with a renegade treasure hunter in hopes of saving Sabrina herself was insane. And yet here she sat because this charismatic, yet dangerous man had convinced her it was the best course of action.

A lump of nausea filled her throat. It was too late. They'd taken off in this noisy, shaking machine bound for Little Eden and the complete unknown. She didn't mind flying. Much. It was the unknown…. And the known. She minded Cade Brock, and she minded the feeling of complete loss of control.

But she didn't have to hand over all the power to him. He still wanted something from her. And she needed to set the ground rules. She'd let him get away with too much already and this whole situation was stringing her nerves so taut, she could hardly stand it.

She opened her eyes and dared a look to her left. The helicopter leveled off and the roar of the engine settled into a dull thrum.

Was Cade really as dangerous as he looked? She lifted her gaze up his broad chest, past the mean scar at his throat, past the tough jaw and un-smiling mouth to… Eyes that nailed her.

"Did I mention I get claustrophobic?" she asked.

"We'll be there soon," he shouted over the noise. "You'll have all the space you want at the villa."

Somehow, she doubted it. Any house with Cade Brock in it would feel like a one-room cabin.

"I'd better have my own room this time."

He seared her with those extraordinary eyes of his. "No problem."

"And I expect transportation back here anytime I say so. I'm giving this a couple of days, tops. Then, whether it gets Sabrina in trouble or not, I'm going to the authorities. I'd rather have her in jail than dead." She bit her lip for a beat. "I mean, not that I think she's done anything wrong." Like set up her own sister to be kidnapped by those goons at the Key Mango apartment last night.

Goons he wanted her to believe were hooked up with Adal Chaba, one of the world's most sought-after terrorist fugitives. She'd recognized his name from the news when Cade had mentioned it. The whole thing was far too incredible. How could Ramiro's globe really contain information that could lead terrorists to clues of the earth's origins? The legends about interstellar visitors leaving the globe behind were ridiculous.

And yet here she sat, with Cade, headed toward Little Eden.

"Right."

She couldn't decide whether he was being sarcastic about Sabrina's innocence or agreeing to transport her back to Marathon at any time of her choosing.

"You have to realize that two days is an unrealistic time frame to search for a shipwreck that hunters have been scouring the ocean for since before either of us was born," she added.

"Technology's a lot more advanced now than in the past. I have the best equipment money can buy. If you can pinpoint the sites, I can find it."

He was nothing if not totally self-assured. Or arrogant. Or not really intending to send her back in two days.

"I can't tell you which one we thought was the *Santa Josefa*," she reminded him. "I can't even tell you if it really *was* the *Santa Josefa*."

He wasn't even looking at her now, his gaze focused on the speeding blur of ocean and sky ahead. "I think you can."

"I guess you just make up your mind how things are going to be and then events fall into place like magic."

"Usually." His voice was so deadpan, she had no idea whether he was kidding. She thought not.

She rolled her eyes and looked out the window at the sheer expanse of blue sea below. They'd left the keys behind quickly and the water rushing by beneath the chopper reminded her of how far outside her comfort zone she was heading with every passing second.

And the fact that she was here at all... Did she *want* to leave her comfort zone?

That thought came unannounced, unintended. It scared her more than the mysterious man sitting way too close beside her.

"Have you forgotten the part about the bad guys who would like to kill you, or worse, that are going to be waiting for you back there?" His deep, hard voice thrummed through the engine noise. Her stomach tightened as more deep blue sea raced by below.

She jerked back to face him.

"Aren't they going to want to kill you if you steal the object for yourself? Say we find it. Say we find Sabrina. She and I head back, free, to North Carolina and leave the globe with you. Isn't someone going to figure out you've got it? What then? Doesn't that make you dead?"

His level, piercing gaze snapped to her again. "I'm not worried about them."

"They almost killed you before."

"Almost is the key word."

"Next time it might not be almost."

"They took me by surprise. Next time, they're the ones who are going to be dead."

Oh, God. Not only was he planning to keep the globe for himself, he was planning to kill anyone else who came after it. And the notion that someone would come after him for it didn't even give him a second's pause.

"You're despicable. You're as bad as they are."

The hard line of his shockingly sexy mouth quirked. "I don't want to blow up the eastern seaboard, Sienna. That might qualify me for a redeeming feature or two."

"I doubt it." Unfortunately, even while she loathed him, she could think of a redeeming feature or two. Or three. Heaven help her. "Just don't forget that you promised you'd help me find Sabrina. This isn't about the damn globe. Not for me."

The dark look he gave her then sent a chill down her spine.

"Finding Sabrina isn't going to be a problem."

Anger surged through her uneasiness. She was really sick and tired of his arrogance and no matter how dangerous it was, she'd go to the police if she had to. "Then what the—"

"Don't you get it yet, Sienna?" he spoke over her, nodding out to the sea whipping by outside the helicopter windows. "She's going to find us."

Chapter 8

The chopper set down on a helipad at the far end of a small island that looked like a verdant crescent from the sky. The concrete pad was surrounded by lush mango, coconut and palm trees. Cade had a Land Rover parked on a dirt road leading up to the helipad and they drove through the pristine wetlands and jungle, the trip to the villa taking less than two minutes.

From what she'd seen from the air, Sienna guessed the island was no more than a half mile wide, maybe three-quarters of a mile long. Birds called from the thick trees and she stepped out of the car into a primeval world where time seemed to stand still.

It was a paradise, and some very deep, very forgotten piece of her heart tightened longingly at the pure sweetness of the air, the crisp scent of the sea, the gentle rushing slide of the ocean hitting the shore somewhere beyond the house.

Cade walked around the side of the Land Rover. The devil walking through heaven as if he'd taken over. Her pulse tripped.

"Welcome to Little Eden," he said.

He stood several feet away from her, though it felt as if he touched her. That was the effect his mere gaze had on her. Her feet rooted to the spot where she stood beside the vehicle. Something about going inside the house felt so difficult, as if crossing the threshold would be the point of no return—when in fact she'd passed the point of no return some time ago.

His unwavering gaze searched hers.

"We have the whole day to work. Let's go inside."

Work. Right. And yet she had the oddest urge to do anything but work here. The island had cast a spell on her already, making the purpose of her tenure on Little Eden hard to remember for a moment. She wasn't here to admire the scenery.

"How long have you owned Little Eden?" she

asked as she followed him up the rock path, then to the wooden steps that led up to the front of the wide-slung villa, much of the front of the house hidden behind foliage that appeared well tended even as it was lazily lush and colorful.

"A few years," he answered briefly.

He opened a box beside the door, pressed his thumb against an unmarked panel, then leaned in for a few seconds. She saw a light flicker then heard a click. He turned the knob and opened the door, waiting for her to enter first.

"Does anyone else live here?" she probed, unsatisfied with his less than generous answer to her first question.

"Not full-time. Staff come in on a scheduled basis for upkeep."

It was evident already that his island home must come with a staff, but they weren't here now, apparently. Yet that, and the high-tech security, fled her mind as she walked inside. Light met her instantly, streaming in from plate glass windows that spanned the entire rear of the house. The entrance flowed into the living area, the floor plan open and spacious, its high ceilings and abundance of natural light lending a luster and depth to the sepia tones of the furnishings that reminded her of a grand old island plantation. Aquamarine, ivory and café au lait shades intermingled with the

rich, natural tones of the walls, ceilings and polished floors like watercolors inspired from the
sea, as if someone—his highly paid decorator, no
doubt—had gathered them up from a deserted
beach and strewn them artfully about the room.

Looking to her left she could see through a set
of French doors to a glasslike pool with a covered
path that led to a small cabana. A hall from the living area led to another part of the house, the bedrooms, perhaps. To the right, the living area opened
through to a dining room with a large rectangular
table that would seat eight, an elegant chandelier
hanging low over it, and beyond, through a wide
arch, she glimpsed a state-of-the-art kitchen.

She resisted the urge to be completely bowled
over by the lavish display of wealth. She had to remember where he'd gotten this wealth—his private island, personal helicopter, luxurious villa.
Treasure not lawfully reported, sold on black mar-
kets, perhaps stolen from other divers, even at gunpoint, if the rumors were true. It was little different
from admiring the plush mansion of a Mafia don.
This type of wealth, this fantasy, was exactly what
had driven her father. What drove Sabrina.

What had destroyed her childhood.

And the very sexy, very tempting, very dangerous man standing behind her was the poster boy
for that high life.

"You must be very proud of your success," she said tensely, turning toward him. "This is quite a house. I'm impressed."

And not in a good way, Cade decided as he watched Sienna turn her vibrant gaze on him, the morning sun and sea through the plate glass windows behind her framing her slender, sexy figure as she faced him.

"It's just a house."

"Oh, come on," she said. "Don't be so modest. This is not just a house. It's every poor wreck diver's dream. It's why they do it."

"That's not true for everyone, Sienna. It's not always about money." He knew her father's death must have turned her against diving, but her intensity still surprised him. What lurked beneath her painful words? He had to remind himself that he was better off not knowing. He didn't want to change her mind about him, or about treasure hunting.

Or maybe he did, to be honest, but he couldn't, no more than he could change her mind about him by explaining that he had good reason to own this house that, despite its outward beauty, was more high-tech compound than vacation beach resort. Every square inch of the small island was monitored by cameras. The house itself was as secure as Fort Knox. His command center, secreted behind a hidden door in the book-lined study, contained a satellite connection to PAX among other things. He worked alone most of the time, but immediate contact, and backup, was at his fingertips. She also couldn't know that locating the *Santa Josefa* wasn't limited by the short time of her two-day limit but rather by her own willingness to remember and pinpoint the wreck. The PAX League's advanced and highly sensitive magnetometers, unavailable to the public, eliminated the possibility of missing the wreck, if only she could narrow down the field of search.

She turned, her gaze catching his across the sunlit room. "A life of leisure earned off the treasures of the sea." The bitter edge to her low voice wasn't lost on Cade. "Do you know how many men ruin their lives trying to get this?"

"You talk about it like it's a sickness."

"Treasure hunting *is* a sickness. It's like gambling. One more roll of the dice..." The darkness in her eyes pierced him uncomfortably. "One more trip out to sea. Steal it if you can't find it. Most people never achieve what you've achieved, though. This island—" She waved back toward the plate glass windows. "This home. It's...amazing."

She didn't sound amazed. She sounded disgusted.

"And I suppose this completes your opinion of me." Now he was the one who sounded bitter, dammit, even to his own ears. She was wrong about him, more wrong than she could imagine. But she was also right. His life was shallow, just not in the way she knew.

"I don't like treasure hunting. I don't like what it does to people, and I don't want any part of it."

"You like it better in your safe little library." He closed the gap between them and she visibly flinched—because of him or his words? He took a guess. "Do you really despise treasure diving, Sienna, or do you fear it? You like to know what's behind every bend in your life, don't you? It drives you crazy that your sister isn't that way, that you can't control her, box her up in your safe world with you. Maybe you're afraid of me, too."

Then he wished he'd kept his mouth shut because those fierce, bright eyes of hers suddenly burned raw with whatever pain she held inside. He wanted nothing more than to reach out and touch her, know again that brief, blinding moment in the lagoon when he'd kissed her and he'd felt oddly whole. It was an unbearable, illogical need, as was this emotional bridge he felt form whenever he looked into her eyes and saw that lurking hurt.

"I'm not afraid of you," she said tightly. "I don't like you. There's a difference."

Her pointed words cut the quiet air inside the villa.

"Then it's a good thing," he said, "that you don't have to."

He stepped back, away from the electric charge of her nearness and the longing building inside him, away from the dark shadow of her eyes. Every minute more he spent with her, he was less sure how to handle her. Less sure he could even handle himself. More sure that even a few days was too long to spend with her and hang on to his sanity. He needed sanity, desperately, just as he needed the ocean. The tightness of his chest wasn't just for the unallowable emotion she evoked in him.

Other than that dip in the lagoon last night, he'd been away from water for almost twenty-four hours, and getting back in it wasn't a choice, but a necessity. Harrison Beck's words reverberated in his head. *You need to come in for more testing.* He knew what those tests would reveal, and he didn't want it confirmed.

He had to live with the fact that sooner or later, if he didn't find the answer he needed, if he didn't get his hands on Chaba, this magnificent villa would be worth about two cents to him.

"While you're on the island," he told Sienna, "please stay inside the house unless you're with me." He led her down the hall, past two closed doors to a third, which he opened. "This is the guest room. Make yourself comfortable. The study is the first door down the hall. Meet me there in an hour."

Cade's arms arced through the clear water, power surging through his body as he melded with the sea, feeling its energy rush through him, fuel him. Then he dove deep with one immense kick. He headed for the depths like a dying man guided by a pinprick of celestial light. He needed this, body and ocean morphing into one, releasing the physical pressure in his chest caused by breathing air directly into his lungs for too long. Here, the oxygen absorbed through his system, relieving the tightness, the tension and the mutation that would eventually kill him unless they found the cure.

The League had never been able to completely dissect the chemical cause of his mutation, though they'd been studying him and testing him since he was six. Chaba had run a biowarfare factory on Valuatu Island before the U.S. had cleared him and his thugs out. There were thousands of species of plants and animals in the jungle rain forests of the island that he could have used to combine with the identifiable chemicals in the bomb. Chaba had managed to sneak out with the materials, only to return and use his weapons against the islanders and humanitarian workers assisting in the postwar cleanup. The mutations suffered by the surviving children had been widely varied, and in many cases not life-threatening.

But in Cade's case, his very existence on ground depended on discovering the secret behind Chaba's bomb. And now, there was a chance he'd find Chaba here, in his world, looking for the *Santa Josefa*.

He couldn't wait. He'd watched his mother and baby brother be blown to pieces before his eyes. He'd run, finally obeying his mother—his delay and his fear costing his family their lives—to the sea, chemicals burning through his skin from the bomb's blast, and dove in.

His life had never been the same, and he couldn't wait for the day that he eliminated the madman who had destroyed his family. He'd see Chaba in hell. That was all that mattered.

I'm not afraid of you. I don't like you.

Sienna's challenging, hurting eyes stormed through his mind, and even here, where he felt more real, more natural, more at home than anywhere, the connection pulled him all the way from Little Eden.

A connection that was as pointless as it was impossible. Even if he ever decided he needed *anyone* in his life, the last person it could ever be was a woman who feared the very thing he needed to survive.

* * *

She'd felt like a total jerk, and then he'd made her feel like a prisoner. *Stay inside the house unless you're with me.* He had told her in the same breath to make herself comfortable. As if that were possible. She was anything but comfortable in Cade Brock's house. Frustrated, Sienna shut the door on the bedroom he'd shown her to and stood there, her nerves bouncing.

Had she hurt his feelings? Did he have feelings? Was it proof she'd lost her mind that she even cared? Had she been completely unfair in her judgment of him?

You like it better in your safe little library.

Yes, yes she did. Edgy, mysterious strangers with dark motives didn't invade her space there. Who was he to psychoanalyze her? And why did it bother her so much that he'd seen right through her bravado to the frightened little mouse hiding inside? There was nothing wrong with being a mouse. Except that maybe she was tired of it. Maybe that was why she was here.

Maybe she really did like him. When she was a teenager, it had been Sabrina who'd hop on the backs of bad boys' motorcycles and roar off into the shadowed streets. Taking off to Little Eden with Cade Brock wasn't much different, only she was old enough to know better. She'd kissed him, slept in the same motel room with him, flown off to a remote island with him... What completely uncharacteristic thing would she do next?

The butterflies flinging themselves against the walls of her stomach weren't entirely unpleasant. She felt an intuitive sexual response every time she looked at him. How in the world could she feel such longing and loathing for the man at the same time?

She didn't know the answer to any of her questions and wasn't entirely sure she wanted to, or that she'd like the answers if she found them.

The wing of the house where the bedrooms were located was isolated, quiet and gorgeous, in a similar weathered seashore palette as the living areas—palest pinks, caramels and creams. Her room had a queen-size bed and goose-down pillows. A chandelier hung here, as well. Translucent ivory drapes pushed back to reveal two sets of French doors that led out to a verdant garden patio. A private bathroom was attached. She set down her small package of toiletries from their convenience store purchases, but realized she wouldn't need them. Anything a guest could require was stocked at the ready in the drawers and cabinets.

She dumped the bag of clothes from the airport boutique on the bed to sort through them. She picked through the items to choose a persimmon tank and a pair of twill shorts, steeled her will, and headed for the door again. Foolish or not, this was the course of action she'd chosen, and she'd handle it, and Cade Brock.

Reaching the study door, she found it locked, and remembered he'd said to meet her in an hour. She knocked, and when there was no answer she wandered into the living area, struck again by how beautiful it was. The house lay in silence around her. Outside, through the huge windows, the ocean rolled, steady and sure. Inside her heart thudded with the endless pull of mystery that Cade Brock inspired.

She wandered into the kitchen, taking in its state-of-the-art appliances and gleaming countertops. In the fridge, she found beer and a half-empty can of beans along with a rotten head of lettuce and some really scary-looking apples that had seen better days.

Perhaps he wasn't such an out-of-the-ordinary man, after all.

The freezer and pantry were better stocked. The dining room, like the kitchen, was supplied with fine tableware and serving pieces. Nothing was dented or dinged and she wondered if he ever used these things. In the trash she found paper plates and plastic cutlery.

Nosy, nosy, nosy. She felt a twinge of guilt as she opened the drawers in the living room, just as she had in the kitchen. It was almost as if the place were a real estate showroom, there was so little of the man who lived here to be revealed.

She wandered back down the hall and stopped at the second door. Knocking lightly, she waited. Then, telling herself that invading his privacy was really okay when her sister's life was at stake, she put her hand on the knob to see if it was kept locked like the study.

The knob turned in her hand. She waited, one second, two, her heart thundering suddenly. No sound. She pushed the door open.

His bedroom lay in shadows, the drapes pulled tightly closed. She reached for the wall switch and light bathed the room. It was almost a match for the bedroom he'd shown her, only slightly larger and with colors more in the sepia shades. There was a large dresser with a scattering of personal items. The wallet she'd gone through last night in the motel bathroom, keys, a few books and several small framed photographs. A young couple with two young boys, maybe four and one.

She recognized Cade's eyes and the shape of his mouth in the oldest boy. He was cute, his eyes bright, his cheeks round and healthy. It was difficult to take her eyes off him, she was so stunned by the image of him as a laughing child, so innocent. The picture was taken on a beach and they were all sitting beneath an oversized umbrella, dressed in swimwear, beaming up at the person taking the photo. Incredibly happy, carefree. She turned the picture over, slid the photograph out of the frame.

There was a handwritten notation on the back—*Valuatu Island, 1975, Mom, Dad, Peter and me.*

She tried to place Valuatu. The Pacific? She wasn't entirely sure, though it pinged somewhere in her memory. Was this where Cade's love of the ocean had begun—he'd grown up around the sea? He had no accent and his parents looked American. What would they have been doing on some far-flung Pacific island? Apparently he had adventure in his blood.

Sliding the photograph back into the frame, she replaced it on the dresser, suddenly remembering that she was snooping and that she didn't have all the time in the world. The digital clock on the bedside table told her it had been forty-five minutes since Cade had told her to meet him in the library. Wherever he'd gone, he'd be back, and soon.

Just another few minutes, that was all she had to find out whatever she could about this stranger in whose hands she'd placed herself and Sabrina. She opened a drawer and pushed aside folded shirts to reach to the back, where she heard something rattle as the drawer slid on its tracks—

A powerful hand clamped down on her arm from out of nowhere. She shrieked as Cade whipped her around and his dark, dangerous gaze caught hers and held as her pulse boomed. She was aware of his heat, his energy, the scent of salt and sea that clung to him. He was wet, she realized wildly. Wet and furious, his fingers biting into her arm, rooting her.

"Curiosity killed the cat." His low voice burned into her. "Don't you know that, Sienna?"

Chapter 9

He watched her eyes, wide and scared and guilty of snooping for his secrets while she was still keeping plenty of her own. She took a deep breath, released it with a soft shudder.

"I'm sorry. I— You weren't in your study and I—"

"Got bored? Thought you'd come find me in my bedroom? Thought maybe I was in my drawer?"

She swallowed visibly, gave a light, tense, fake shrug.

"Oh, you know, the eternal question. Boxers or

briefs." She laughed in a brittle way and he didn't let go of her arm when she tried to move.

"Interested in my underwear, Sienna?" He watched her cheeks bloom a light pink. "You only had to ask."

A tingling buzz at the base of his spine told him just how difficult it would be for him to say no if she did. The heavy flow of blood in his veins revealed all too well how much he wanted her in his bed, how quickly his irritation was changing into something else.

That would be a mistake, and maybe he had to show her that, or maybe he had to show himself, but he knew he had to make sure this was the last place she came sneaking around to again.

Boldly, he moved his other hand to her waist, felt the soft, strong curve of her body. He slid his touch upward, grazing past the side of her breast as he slipped his arm around her back and tugged her close, hot against him. Her cheeks flushed deeper and she pushed with the flat of her free hand against his chest.

"You said you didn't take women against their will," she said, panic tingeing her voice.

"You're in my bedroom," he reminded her.

"That was a mistake. I was looking for my room. I opened the wrong door."

"Stick your hand in a dark hole, don't be sur-

prised if you find something that hurts you,"
he said.

"Are you going to hurt me?"

God, he hoped not. What he really wanted to do
was pull her all the way into his arms and kiss her
then take her to bed, whether it was wrong or not.

But what he *needed* was for her to tell him everything she knew about the *Santa Josefa*. He
needed for her to start trusting him.

He let her go so suddenly, she stumbled a bit
as she took a huge step back. He reached his hand
in the damn drawer, pulled out a silver object and
slammed it on the dresser.

"Is this what you wanted to see? It was my
brother's baby rattle."

She blinked and said nothing for a taut beat.
"Peter?" she whispered starkly.

He ignored the tight grind in his gut. She'd tak-
en the photograph out of the frame and read the in-
scription on the back, that was the only explanation.
"He's dead," he said. "It's the only thing of his I
have left to remember him by—when I want to remember, which mostly I don't. You see, I know
what it feels like to lose the people you love." He
tamped down the painful swell in his throat. "Satisfied now, Sienna? Curiosity appeased?"

Her eyes shadowed. "I'm s—"

He cut her off, dismissed her. "I'm going to

shower and change. This time, I'd appreciate it if you actually met me in the study."

And he'd appreciate it even more if she ran the hell out of his room before he lost the control he was famed for owning.

She did.

She found him ten minutes later unlocking the study, his mouth grim, whatever was going through his mind more than what he'd told her in his bedroom. There was tragedy in his past, now she knew. Her snooping had uncovered that much, and she wished it hadn't.

It was one thing to be aware of the undeniable attraction she felt for him, and quite another to let him touch her emotions. It made him more complicated, more real.

He ushered her inside the room, which was as richly appointed as the rest of the house, only her mind immediately prevented any notice of the fine furnishings as she took in what he had spread out on the large desk.

"Oh, my God," she breathed. "These are originals, aren't they?" He had *original* Spanish charts and maps and— "This…"

"Is a gold disk from the *Caravilla*." He moved behind her to the desk, came over to where she stood. Her hand hovered over the exquisite engraved disk he had left laid casually on the desk like a cheap paperweight. "You can touch it."

She was almost scared to, but God, she wanted to. The *Caravilla* was a Spanish galleon from the 1700s, one of the sister ships of the *Santa Josefa*.

Her fingers burned. Her pulse pounded. It was the same breathless energy she remembered from so many years ago when she'd plucked her first piece of eight from the bottom of the sea. The shock and thrill of sweeping away sea grass and sand, never knowing what might lie beneath. *Treasure.* Wondering what daring captain might last have touched it.

Of course, in truth, finding real treasure meant months and years of work and research and money, of danger. Her father had operated on hope and a prayer most of the time, the occasional streak of luck keeping them going from summer to summer when he'd quit whatever temporary job he'd taken over the winter to bring his family back to the sea. Hunting with old and inadequate equipment because he couldn't afford better. Selling whatever he found to keep them afloat.

She looked up at the bookshelves lining the room up to the ceilings and realized they were filled not just with an amazing collection of maritime history books but with treasures, just sitting there, like other people placed trinkets from home decorating stores. A glass vase filled with gold doubloons. An antique musket. A brass keyplate, a framed frayed and discolored chart of a French treasure ship, silver wedges, porcelain figures and even a cannonball, still partially encrusted, placed on the floor like a doorstop. Photographs of Cade with various crews on dives, holding up finds.

Cade's brooding eyes met hers as she slowly turned back to him where he stood, too near. The mysterious intensity of his gaze defined him somehow, and her heartbeat sped.

"I just need a chart I can mark," she said, pulling back, away from the gold disk, the ancient map, everything that she knew he'd set out deliberately to tempt her. This world of his was a world she'd left behind, for her own sanity.

"You feel it, don't you?" he asked quietly.

Roaring heartbeat? Heating blood? Oh, she felt it, but then she knew that wasn't what he meant.

"I'm not interested in treasure. I'm interested in finding the *Santa Josefa* and saving Sabrina's life." And trying to stay alive in the meantime, and whole.

"You had the fever once, didn't you? The treasure fever? The call of the hunt?"

"I agreed to mark a chart for you, that's all. You have a crew of your own, I assume."

He didn't say anything. Dammit. She'd had her suspicions all along that he intended to pressure her to help him. He wouldn't trust a hired crew to go after the *Santa Josefa*. And he wasn't doing anything now to allay those suspicions. But he couldn't possibly understand how sick it made her feel in the pit of her stomach to think of going out on the sea with him, much less diving under.

Could she do it? Her mouth dried and her pulse quickened again. She hadn't thought of diving in years, hadn't wanted to. She didn't even swim, not anymore.

Can't swim or won't swim? he'd demanded. Her stomach clenched and she pushed the question away.

Walking around the desk, he pulled out a rolled map, a crisp, contemporary chart, and, pushing aside the ancient one as if it weren't worth thousands of dollars, he spread it on the desk and sat.

What money could buy a treasure hunter bowled her over yet again. Her father would have been in heaven right here in this study on Little Eden with its satellite-generated, wreck diver's dream materials.

Her father's sun-weathered face and shining eyes filled her mind, and a sharp pain stabbed her chest. They'd been down to their last dime that summer, as usual. They were always on their last dime, and somehow her father always found one more to keep his beat-up boat afloat.

Then— *Blood.*

Sienna felt her knees shake as she sat down in the padded leather chair in front of the desk and reached with shaking fingers for the pen he'd laid down atop the crisp, high-tech chart.

"Are you all right?"

"I'm fine." She had to be fine.

She thought about the chart she'd found in Sabrina's apartment instead, shut her eyes and focused on visualizing the spots marked in her father's broad scrawl. The marks were burned into her mind. Shock, horror. She'd known Sabrina was in trouble even then. She just hadn't realized how much.

"Here. And here." She opened her eyes quickly and jabbed the pen at coordinates off the middle keys. "This isn't exact, but pretty close. You'd have to get out there and do a grid search. These were just locations he wanted to return to. We didn't hit all of them that summer."

She looked up at him. "A couple of them he'd learned about from fishermen who'd seen something that made them think there were wrecks in these areas, and others he'd probably picked up from the grapevine. Someone had found a piece of gold, or a cannon, then lost the site and Dad was going to go back to investigate."

"The *Santa Josefa* would have been the biggest find of his life," Cade said.

"Maybe he'd still have a life if he hadn't been treasure hunting." Sienna looked away from his dark, searching gaze. She stabbed at the map again, marking several more areas. Then the final three spots.

"We weren't equipped for deep-water excavation," she pointed out. "He would have left those for last, or tried to get another team to help us, and we were out alone that day, I know that, just the three of us." Nausea rose, burned, and she took a deep breath. "I really don't know what you're going to do with this information. You'd need to start with a seaplane, do an aerial survey, and God knows sand is shifting all the time, the wreck could have moved from the currents—"

"Do you remember how much of the coast you could see from the boat that day? How far off from shore you were? Any landmarks that stood out?"

"No, I don't remember! Do you think I'm lying?" She felt sweat pop out on her brow. "When I woke up in the hospital, I couldn't remember anything that had happened. I asked for my father." Her throat choked. "They had to tell me what had happened."

"Tell me," he said, and his voice was gentle enough to nearly break her control.

"I have to go now." She had to go throw up, if she wasn't lucky. She had to get away from his sympathetic eyes that tore at her and made her feel even more vulnerable than these damn charts and her memories of that fatal summer. "You're on your own. I told you this was all I could do."

She rose and moved, blindly, for the study door.

He was behind her so quickly she didn't even hear him, only felt him, the whisper of air as he reached past her and slammed his hand against the study door, blocking her between the closed door and his hard body.

"You need to get back in the water, Sienna. I know you're afraid, but fear feeds on itself. Stop feeding it."

"I don't need to do anything." She refused to turn, refused to look at him. *Fear feeds on itself.* Did he think she didn't know that? Was that little homily supposed to solve everything?

His low voice slid through the fiery panic waving over her. "They could beat us to the *Santa Josefa.* Your father died a long time ago, but Sabrina is still alive. I need you to come with me. We don't have much time."

Guilt. God, the guilt could crush her. She was weak, and he was piercing her with the knowledge that her weakness could hurt Sabrina now.

"I don't know what makes you think that my getting in the water again is going to save Sabrina's life or make me remember which one of those sites we were searching that last day." She turned and pushed at his immovable chest. "Take your hand off the door."

He stood there with his feet firmly planted inches in front of her, his powerful arm stretched out over her shoulder, his palm flat against the door behind her.

"It's worth a try, isn't it? For Sabrina?"

For Sabrina. "You mean for you. You don't give a damn about Sabrina."

"But you do, don't you, Sienna? You care."

"You act like it's just a choice! I choose not to remember. I choose not to swim. I would have died in that lagoon if you hadn't dragged me out of it. It's not a choice. I have anxiety attacks! And I have medication for it, but I lost it in my damn bag in Key Mango! Are you happy now?"

She blinked fast, stared down at her feet, his feet right in front of them. *Do not throw up right here.* Or faint. God, her heart was beating so fast—

All of it, Sabrina, the maps, the treasure sitting around Cade's office, the dark, frightening shadow of the past lurking hidden and yet so painful in her mind—

A warm touch lifted her chin. A surprisingly gentle touch. Her emotions were so conflicted, she didn't know what she was feeling.

She hated this man, hated everything he stood for.

And yet some incomprehensible connection seized her, and even if she weren't trapped here between his strong body and the door of his study, she knew she wouldn't have moved. It was like an invisible thread held her.

His eyes were steady, safe now. Not pushing her anymore.

Just…concerned, damn him.

"I'm sorry," he said.

She felt something wet splash down her cheek. Oh, God, she was crying. In front of him. She wasn't even sure what he was apologizing for.

"Just leave me alone," she whispered thickly. "I can't help you. You were wrong if you thought I could. I can't help Sabrina either."

She took a ragged breath and prayed he'd let the matter drop. Prayed he'd let her run away and hide, because that was all she wanted to do. She wanted to run right back to her safe little library. Only right now, there could be a killer or two waiting for her there, and she was stuck with Cade Brock on Little Eden.

Her chest ached as though it had been turned inside out, the way her life had been.

He moved, stepped back. She put her shaking hand on the knob and opened the door.

Behind her, she heard him speak.

"I know you think you're right, Sienna. But what if you're the one who's wrong?"

Chapter 10

He'd pushed her too far, or not far enough. He wanted her to be just another tool, a thing he used to complete his mission. But his conscience stabbed him as he shut and locked the study door behind her, stabbed him just the way her amber eyes had.

She was a woman trapped in a hurt so deep, she'd blocked it in some kind of trauma-induced amnesia. And here he was, trying to force her into the very thing that horrified her most.

Alone, he crossed the room to press the hidden latch that released one wall of shelves. Inside the private study annex, he sat behind another desk and flicked the mouse to bring up the screen that connected him to PAX, then turned to the fax machine to lift out a scan of Sabrina Parker's North Carolina driver's license. Beneath it, the tray held a series of scanned documents—her birth certificate, school records, passport, tax returns. He flipped through the stack to find identical documentation on Sienna. The League's investigators had been busy.

Neither of the women had criminal records, and nothing in Sabrina's background contained any suspicious activity. She'd carefully utilized her Tabitha Donovan identity, and further documents showed the exact same face on a passport for Tabitha Donovan. Sabrina had taken a sabbatical from her university position and in a blink had turned into Tabitha, leaving her squeaky clean marine archaeology professorship behind.

Had she planned to return to it at all? She'd lied thoroughly, even to her twin sister… For Sienna's protection, or so she could use her? He still believed she'd called Sienna and gotten her out to Key Mango as a decoy.

Meanwhile, Tabitha Donovan had vanished.

He logged into the system, then sent a scan of the chart as marked by Sienna. The League could get some aerials to him by tomorrow, but he wasn't waiting for them. There was no time to waste. The weather patterns were ominous for the late afternoon, and he was determined to get a head start today.

Going back to the outer office, he shut up the wall of shelves and went back to compare Sienna's markings on the new map with the period chart. Skirting the keys and the dangerous reefs near shore, the *Santa Josefa* had been headed back to Spain when it encountered three days of heavy seas and storms that had sent it off course. On October 3, 1739 it had hit a submerged rock, revealing that it had been closer to land than the captain had planned. Leaking badly, the ship had floundered for several days while the crew worked to keep the galleon afloat to survive. They feared the storm would tear their dinghies apart if they attempted to get to shore, but eventually took the chance when the exhausted crew could no longer pump.

How far back out to sea the ship had floated after it had hit the rock was the great unknown. A handful of the *Santa Josefa*'s crew had made it to shore, picked up a week later by a sister ship that had managed to steer clear of the storm's rage.

Survivor reports indicated they'd been picked up on one of the smaller islands in the middle keys. That, along with the fact that the ship had struck a submerged rock, had led searchers for years to hunt the shallow waters along the middle keys, to no avail.

Very likely, Cade's instincts and experience told him, it was in deeper water. If it had lain in one of the coastal sites Sienna had marked, it would have been found already. The shallow waters along the keys were among some of the most explored shipwreck hunting grounds in the world. Her father would have started there first then moved on. And the fact that he hadn't been equipped for deep-water excavation wouldn't have stopped him if he'd been keen on discovering the legendary Ramiro's globe, a find that alone would be worth millions. It could be brought up by hand, no heavy machinery required.

Chaba's men would most likely begin their search with the shallower sites due to the easier access. But eventually, they too would come to the conclusion that the deeper water sites were the key. Cade might be wrong, but if he was right, he could get there first. Once he had the globe, he'd have exactly what Chaba wanted.

And since Chaba had something he wanted… It was a dangerous game. There was no way he'd turn the globe over to Chaba, not even to save his own life.

But that was the next phase. First he had to find

the globe, which would be a hell of a lot easier if he had the secrets hiding in Sienna's mind.

Nothing else had made his radar in years other than completing the next mission and using anyone he had to in order to get the job done. But he was tied up in knots over what he was putting Sienna through, and that said more about the impact she was having on him than he wanted to know.

Pale skin marked by a vivid bruise and huge eyes stared back at Sienna from the mirror of the bathroom. She looked like hell. She looked scared out of her mind.

It was this damn island, the artifacts and maps, the ocean surrounding her, taunting her, just outside the villa. And Cade Brock, most of all Cade Brock. She didn't want to think about any of it, and now she couldn't stop.

Her mother had gone into a dramatic decline after Sienna's father had died. Mentally, Nora Parker had gone straight to hell with a bottle. Maybe if Sienna was honest just a little, she'd admit her mother had always been a drunk. She'd just taken to it like a mission in widowhood. She'd gone back and forth between rehab centers and psychiatric hospitals until she'd taken off with her suspended license and driven her car the wrong way down an off-ramp. Sienna and Sabrina had been

taken in by an aunt who hadn't much wanted two
new teenage daughters, having just gotten her own
children out of college and off on their own.

Sienna had spent the next several years con-
vincing herself she wasn't as crazy as her mother
just because she'd lost an entire summer of her
memory. She didn't need alcohol or a clinical psy-
chiatrist. She started refusing to talk to the doctors her aunt took her to. She just threw herself
into her studies, her work, the controlled life she'd
built around herself like the Berlin Wall. She had
her anti-anxiety medication to keep her sane when
the panic got out of hand.

Now she had nothing, nothing but herself in the
mirror. And what she saw was a coward who
wanted to run away and hide.

What if you're the one who's wrong?

She left the bathroom, strode to the door and
flung it open. She didn't think. She was afraid to
think. That little ball of panic in her stomach was
just waiting for her to think so it could explode.

The living area lay quiet in the bright midday
light. There was no sign of Cade, and God, she
didn't want a sign of Cade. She had to do this
alone. No witnesses. Because maybe she wasn't
wrong at all.

French doors in the kitchen led to the rear pergola. Screw Cade Brock and his orders for her to

stay inside. She wasn't his prisoner. If he wanted to issue challenges, he'd have to take the consequences.

Fine wrought iron chairs sat waiting around a glass-topped table. The steps down to the beach were wooden and hot beneath her bare feet. She tasted salt in the air as she reached the sand, white and fine and burning against her skin.

The light breeze kicked her hair across her cheeks, and her pulse rocked hard in her veins. No panic, no panic. Deep breaths. The packed sand near the shore was firm beneath her feet even as she felt the world inside her head rock. She swallowed tightly and inhaled the sharp, salty air she knew so well.

The soothing, repetitive rush of the tide hummed in her ears. For a moment, she allowed herself to simply stare out at the undulating water. Wasn't this what the doctors had wanted her to do, years ago? Get back in the water? Damn Cade Brock for being right about that, too.

She closed her eyes and took another step, deliciously warm liquid sliding over her toes. She remembered impossibly clear seas, these very waters off the keys, where she swam her childhood away like a fish who'd found home. Deeper, deeper, where the sun no longer penetrated, to the cool, vast blue beneath it all, a world of soundless freedom where she'd frolicked like a mermaid.

A sliding sensation of long-lost joy spun through her blood, tangling with the twist of fear. There *had* been good times. How had she forgotten that? She took another step, felt the water lap her ankles. Opening her eyes, she realized she was smiling and crying all at the same time. It wasn't much of anything, just a step in the surf. But somehow it felt so much bigger because she was still standing there.

She stretched out her arms and, God, she might not be able to imagine diving, but for a heart-tangling beat, she was damn sure she could fly.

Cade watched her through the plate glass windows of the living area, startled by the sight of Sienna Parker standing in the surf, hair blowing around her, arms outstretched. Then she spun, her light, willowy figure like a siren in the sea, enchanting and drawing him. He didn't move, didn't even breathe, just stared, mesmerized by what he realized instinctively was some kind of very private ritual. He fought his instinct to bang outside and order her in, safe from the exposure of the beach. He didn't know what had moved her—his challenge, her sister's fate, or her own need to face her fear. Self-torture, or self-therapy.

A distant beating sound thrummed through the still house, spiking fire in his veins. He raced to the door and ran outside. Her face lifted, her gaze sparked into his.

Goddammit. He didn't have time to look back. The sound of a helicopter rushing closer roared in his ears.

Fear beyond what he'd expected iced his blood. If this was someone checking out the possibility that it could have been Cade Brock in Key Mango, Cade Brock who'd taken off with someone who looked just like Tabitha/Sabrina— He couldn't let her be seen on his island.

"Get in the house," he roared.

Sienna froze then started to move, but not fast enough. In another beat the craft would be directly over them and all he had time to do when he reached her was hit the sand, pushing her down, covering her body with his.

He held her tightly, safely, in his arms, her slender body shaking under him. And he did the one thing he, the playboy billionaire, would be doing if he'd brought a lady love back to his private island for a romantic getaway. A playboy billionaire who didn't have terrorists and the *Santa Josefa* on his mind. He crushed his mouth over hers.

Shock held Sienna immobile for a moment then she opened her mouth to scream, but it was swallowed by Cade's tender assault. He stroked his tongue along hers in erotic invitation and all she could do was dig her fingers into his shoulders and kiss him back.

He rocked against her, melting her bones and her brain into the sand as he devoured her. Finally he let go, and she stared up at him, breathless. Her pulse hummed and her limbs tingled. Somewhere above, the beating of the chopper that had been coming over the beach still pounded, but not nearly as loud as the blood pounding in her ears.

There was a grim look in his eyes warring with something deeper, something wild that she felt, too.

She opened her mouth again, to say what, she didn't know, but he touched her lips with his finger, then slowly, achingly slowly, he took her lips again and she couldn't have stopped him to save her life. She didn't *want* to stop him. Her lashes fell shut again and she could have crawled up his body and hung on forever. She needed, wanted, more. More of his mouth plundering hers, more of his lean power crushing her breasts against his hard chest, more of this shocking need, more of the life-giving sweetness of his kiss….

He lifted his mouth from hers again, and she opened her eyes, met his stunningly hot gaze an inch away. Shocking awareness left her shaking. There was no sound now but wind and tide.

"It's safe now," he said, his voice husky, low

and with just enough of a shake that she knew he'd been hit hard, too.

Safe. The word danced around her dizzied brain as he moved off her, reached down and pulled her to her feet.

"Safe from what?"

"I told you to stay inside," he reminded her, his voice tight as he controlled it. "You can be seen here on the beach, from the sea, from the sky. That could have been them. Could have been a tourist chopper. I don't know."

That was why— Oh, God, that was why he'd kissed her. He'd been playing a game, a charade, lovers on the beach, hiding her appearance from the possible spying eyes overhead.

She swallowed thickly, felt the tears she'd cried in the surf still wet on her cheeks. Her lips still burning from his kiss. Her entire body shaking from the tangle of it all. She wanted to be angry, but she didn't know what she felt now. She just knew she was in no shape for rational thought and she was a little afraid of anything she might say now.

"I came outside to—" She felt the sting of emotion again, the sting of stupid hurt that he hadn't kissed her for any other reason than to hide her identity. Though when she looked at him now, she wasn't sure that was true. The heat in his eyes told her a different story, the same story the passion in his kiss had, but she wasn't sure it mattered or if she could figure out how it did. Didn't she have enough turmoil without blowing a kiss out of proportion? She turned away. "I'm sorry." She felt stupid.

"I'm not."

She looked back at him. Wind whipped at her, and she pushed the hair out of her eyes. He stood there, solid as a rock.

"I know you're strong, and now so do you," he said.

She felt a sting behind her eyes again. "You don't know me at all."

He reached up and touched her face, rubbed the tip of his finger across the dried track of her tear. "I know you better than you think I do. I know what it feels like to lose your family, Sienna. I know that fear and guilt can freeze a person. I know that the only way past it is to do the thing that scares you the most, whether you want to or not."

For a long moment, his touch lingered on her cheek and she let the strange comfort of him, the man she didn't trust and could swear she hated, fill her.

Wind lashed at her cheeks, stinging her eyes. She felt him drop his fingers from her cheek, then he closed his hands over hers. "He saved my life, you know?" she whispered. "He got the shark away from me and he— When I woke up in the hospital, they told me my father was dead. He died to save me."

Cade's grip closed tighter over her hand.

She blinked several times, fighting back more tears, wishing she really was strong, and somehow feeling stronger because Cade told her he thought she was.

"I just never wanted to go back in the water again," she said thickly, turning her gaze from him to the sea. "You asked me if I can't swim or won't swim. I don't even know anymore. I think I forgot what it felt like to want to, even. My parents— They weren't real happy. My father was completely addicted to hunting for treasure. I think my mother thought it ruined her life. After my father died, she drove the wrong way on an off-ramp, drunk." She bit her lip, fighting down the choked feeling in her throat, staring down at the gritty sand at her feet now, the sound of the tide storming like her heart. She lifted her gaze to Cade finally. "I just always wanted a normal life. I wanted to forget it all, let go of it all."

"That's not letting go, Sienna," he said gently. "That's hanging on."

She swallowed thickly. He was right, damn

him. But she wasn't sure how to let go. And she wasn't angry, just a little scared.

"I don't like being afraid."

"Then come with me," he said, taking both her hands in his now. "You don't have to dive. Just come with me on the boat, and let go."

She felt the hot sand beneath her feet, the cool kiss of the salt breeze, the painful pull of the truth about herself. She looked into his eyes, and knew he was right, that somewhere out there was the thing that had been locking her up in a prison of her own making for half her life. "Okay."

Chapter 11

A trio of cranes dove, swooped, then rose up again from the water, fish dangling from their beaks. Dark gray clouds rimmed the horizon, threatening a late-day storm.

The teasing breeze carried no hint of the rain to come as Cade slowly ran straight lines back and forth across the target area for the third mark of the day. They'd been out for hours, and had found nothing. They'd lunched on sandwiches and cold drinks from a cooler. He kept asking her if she was all right.

She didn't know the answer.

A side-sonar pen traced patterns of the sea floor

while a computer sent up ghostly images from the seabed. Waves lapped the boat's hull as Cade cut the engine.

"There's something down there," he said.

Voices from the past pricked her mind. *There's something down there, Nora.* Her father's excitement never went away, every new find just as thrilling as the last. But this one had been different. *This is it. Our life's going to change, Nora. You'll see. We're gonna be rich. Water streamed off her father as he stood on the foredeck of their beat-up boat. Pride and hope filled Sienna's heart, then she looked at her mother. Fear marked Nora's eyes.*

Horror movie reels twisted in Sienna's mind. Blood, so much blood. Sienna slammed her hand to her mouth, and she staggered on the rolling deck.

It's not worth it, Clifton. They aren't going to give up.

Shut up, Nora. The Santa Josefa *is mine! We'll beat them. I have a plan.*

Junk, nets full of it, seared into Sienna's mind. *We'll beat them, we'll beat them.*

She couldn't breathe. She was going to choke. The anxiety attack struck full force.

"Sienna."

Sweat, chills.

"I can't do this," she said thickly. "We have to go back." Her teeth rattled.

His hard eyes gentled on her. He knelt in front of her, rubbed her chill-bumped arms. "You don't have to do anything. You don't have to go down there."

Memories, chopped and mixed up, sliced through her mind. Water, danger. Deep, dark. Blood. Men coming at them with guns.

Sharks. They'd been attacked by sharks. What men with guns? Her mind spun.

She was scared to death.

"I don't think you should go down there," she said sharply.

Shaking. She was shaking all over.

"You need to sit down." He guided her back to the bench seat. "It's okay, Sienna. I'm an expert diver."

"So was my father. He died."

Deep breaths. She needed to take deep breaths. Cade's eyes on her, fathomless and direct, made her dizzy. "There aren't any sharks here today, Sienna. We're here. I'm going to check it out."

She wasn't going to be able to stop him. He grabbed a bottle of water from the cooler and brought it back to her. "I won't stay down long, I promise. Forty-five minutes." He tapped her watch. "You can time me."

She didn't pick up the bottle of water.

He was dressed in boat trunks and a T-shirt. The warm waters off the keys didn't require a wet suit, but he had everything else and more. She hadn't been in a boat since she was seventeen years old and while some of the equipment and instruments he'd rigorously checked before they set out were familiar, much of it was unfamiliar—including some expensive-looking electronic gadgets. Her father had certainly never been equipped with anything like it.

A wild flood of sensations whipped through her as she watched him check his dive watch, reach for his tank. She glanced over the bridge to the wind gauge.

He slipped his arms into the nylon shoulder straps of the backpack that would accommodate his air tank and picked up his weight belt.

The routine was achingly familiar, coming back to her in shots of adrenaline as she watched him check each tool as he loaded it in the bag— knife, dive light, shears, retractor. If she wanted to go with him, he had a crew's worth of gear in the closed compartments he'd gotten his from. He had long-range, deadly looking spear-guns that had made her heart trip when she'd spied them.

Did he use those for fish?

There was a rifle on the bridge, too.

Almost completely fitted out, he checked the compass bearings once more against the charts, and made another depth reading before striding across the deck. He targeted the tip of a rock projection off a reef in the distance as a gunsight. When he returned, he slung a pair of binoculars on the bench seat beside her.

"Forty-five minutes," he promised again. "The wind's picking up. The storm's moving in." His face was tense. "We don't know what's going on with the people who were looking for Sabrina, if they've found her by now."

They would be looking for the *Santa Josefa,* too. And the delay caused by the incoming storm would give them time to get here. Time to search the sites before Cade could if they didn't take this opportunity.

She drew in a shuddering breath as he pulled on his flippers.

"Be careful," she said.

His mouth quirked sexily. "I'm always careful, Sienna."

She didn't know if she believed that. He had this invincible quality to him, but sharks weren't all they had to worry about.

He donned his mask and executed a smooth pike dive into the water.

* * *

The water cooled as he descended, but remained comfortable. Cade streamed downward, kicked hard to increase his speed. Fish darted out of his way.

He didn't need the tank on his back or the weight belt strapped to his middle. He had all of this equipment and more for when he went out with teams from the keys, acquaintances he talked up, drank with in bars, to keep the chain of information flowing when he worked a case. All the people he lied to on a daily basis without caring a whit.

Above, he'd left behind a woman he cared way too much about lying to.

There were a million reasons things would never work between the two of them. Maybe she was working on overcoming her fear of the water. Maybe she could even, eventually, be tempted back into treasure hunting. She had the fire, the fever, even if she didn't want to admit it.

But she would never accept that he was the man who would put her sister behind bars.

And the truth about his mutation...

Even the loving adoptive parents who had taken him home after the Valuatu Island bombing had rejected him, turned him over to the League, frightened of their strange little boy and the prognosis for his future. Since then, the secrecy required of him had kept his powers under wraps. Under the sea.

Alone, as he reached the seafloor, he quickly unbuckled the straps, dropped the tank and mask and hoses. Ripped off the weight belt.

He was free. This was his world.

Lilac sea fans spread out around him, undulating gently in the dark water. He didn't need the dive light to see them. He left that behind with the useless gear and checked his dive watch. Forty-five minutes, he'd promised Sienna. She would worry if he was down one heartbeat longer.

And that she would worry about him was something he couldn't dwell on, not now. He had work to do.

He headed for the hull sticking out of the sand. It was completely encrusted, the wood long ago eaten away. But was it the three-hundred-year-old hull of the *Santa Josefa?* As he neared, he pushed the sea grasses aside, swishing a school of silver minnows out of his way. Whatever this had been, it had broken up over a wide path. A discoloration in the sand drew him to the side of the coral-consumed hull and he darted toward it, rubbing the sand aside to uncover something round.

A bronze porthole.

He frowned and dug his knife into the sand below it. Found a metal object, pulled it, but it didn't budge. Using the tool, he worked at it steadily, quickly, and already he had the sinking feeling in his stomach that this wasn't the *Santa Josefa*. Not with that bronze porthole.

It took several more minutes to pry the object loose. He brushed away the silt. He was holding a ship's telegraph. Most likely, what he had here was a World War II merchant transport carrier.

He swam on, gliding just above the seabed, kicking slowly, stopping occasionally to dig in a hole or push aside the grasses, finding more evidence of the same. Numerous merchant ships had sunk in these waters in the last hundred years, and everything about this site was telling him that was what his readings had picked up.

The *Santa Josefa* was still out there, somewhere.

A dark dot on the horizon was her first clue.

Sienna picked up Cade's binoculars and focused on the boat slicing through the choppy water, headed straight for the cabin cruiser sitting at anchor.

The boat was small, and there were two men… Two men with rifles.

Her heart bounced straight up into her throat. *Sit tight, Nora. They'll go away. Then it will be ours.*

The men pulled alongside their boat. Got anything today, Parker?

Just a pile of junk down there.

Blood.

Sienna squeezed her eyes shut, fought back the

panic, the confusing slices of memory, and slammed the binoculars down to look at her watch. Twenty minutes. Cade had only been down for twenty minutes.

In another twenty, that boat would be on top of them. She stumbled across the rolling deck for Cade's rifle. She could protect herself, or she could at least try.

There were two of them and one of her. Even if she was able to aim and take out one of them, the other one would blow her head off, and all before Cade came back up.

Then they'd go down after him. They'd kill him. *They'd kill him like they killed her father.*

Shock strummed through her system. She felt as if her mind was breaking apart into puzzle pieces she didn't know how to put together. Her father had been killed by a shark, but she was remembering another team of hunters. She was shaking so badly she didn't feel her legs move when she stood. Deep breaths, that was all she could focus on. Don't think. She couldn't think anymore or she wouldn't be able to do this.

Her stomach dipped and fear ripped through her in one cold shot.

She would have died in that lagoon without Cade because of this panic of hers, this blind fear of water. Or would she? If he hadn't been there, would her instincts have kicked in? Surely survival would have won out.

Would she let these men kill her before she'd jump back in the water to warn Cade so they could get out of here?

She didn't have time to throw up. She would either do this, or she would die, and so would he. She stumbled across the deck again, threw open the gear compartment. Backpack, air tank—filled already, thank God. Regulator, masks, fins. She moved automatically, fighting back those nightmare pieces pushing at the edges of her consciousness. Pushing them away before she went crazy.

The edge of the boat felt strange and the floating sensation of dropping off a high-rise building swept over her as she rolled backward into the water.

Her mind raced as the silent world of the sea enveloped her. The world above was a blur of hazy light and below, a seemingly bottomless abyss waited. Pain rocked her, and terror had her clawing upward. Her ears, God, it was her ears. She struggled through the pain to clear them and stay under.

She *remembered* how to clear them.

The terror subsided with the pain. Instinct. Rely on instinct. Her mantra. She could do this. Or she would die. Two choices. She knew which one she was making, and even as the thought settled in her mind, a sense of pride and achievement came with it.

But there was no time to enjoy it. And the ball of panic wasn't far away. She couldn't do this for long or she'd risk panicking.

If you're going to panic, you have no business diving. Her father's voice roared in her mind, followed by slicing horror clips. Blood. The mouth of the shark coming at her—

She realized she was holding her breath, a mistake, and she forced herself to inhale and exhale, evenly, shoving the terrible images from her mind as she kicked downward. There were no sharks here.

There were sharks above, possibly, in that boat coming toward Cade's cabin cruiser. That was all she could allow herself to think.

The seafloor seemed to rise up toward her rather than her descending to it. The dive light she had, thank God, remembered to grab strobed across the coral and shells and knocked into the hull shape she'd seen on the screen in the boat. She touched bottom, began to move toward the hull, tripped over something and looked down.

Cade's air tank, belt, mask… All of his gear.

Oh, God. New horror ripped through her.

He was dead. Oh, God. He was dead. Her mind screamed. She whipped around, streaking the light through the surreal dark underworld.

Nothing. She saw nothing. But something had happened to Cade, something had… What? Torn him to shreds, eaten him whole, spit out his gear? That didn't make sense, but she was beyond sense.

She streaked upward, panic taking over.

Something grabbed her waist and she knew she was going to die, too.

Chapter 12

She fought him hard, as if she were fighting for her life. And he had no doubt she thought she was. But he was fighting for her life, too, and if she kept shooting up this way, she could die.

He pulled her against his chest, banding her with his arms so she couldn't move, had no choice.

She'd left him with no choice either. But first he had to get her back to the surface alive.

Twisting her, he met her shattered eyes. The fear there was no less than the fear he'd seen through the water below as he watched her discover his gear. And now… Now she'd discovered more.

She froze for an awful moment, the horror in her eyes slashing into his chest. He didn't know if she didn't believe what she was seeing, or if she was just so terrified she didn't know what she was seeing.

He pulled her up with him, streaming slowly, the rise controlled, safe, and then as soon as he let go, she reared out of the water ahead of him, tore up the ladder, fell into the boat.

A dark streak in the sea grabbed his eye. He jumped into the boat.

"They're coming after us," she gasped, tearing off the mask, ripping off the gear. "They're going to kill us!"

He reached for the binoculars, veins thundering. Now he knew what had pushed her into the water after him. The figures in the boat came into focus.

He tossed the binoculars down. "I've worked with those men. They're friends of mine. They're no terrorists. They're hunters, just like me."

Sienna grabbed hold of the railing as the cruiser rolled under her feet.

"Just like you?" she gasped. Her face was white, her limbs shaking, and from more than the exertion. "What are you, Cade?"

He took a step toward her. Wind whipped hair into her face and her hand shook as she slashed at it. He'd told her plenty of lies, but there were no lies that could cover what she'd seen.

"I'm just a man, Sienna." That much was true. And he couldn't lose her yet. Couldn't lose her to fear. He still needed her help to find the *Santa Josefa.* Needed her trapped memories.

"You're not a man. Men can't breathe underwater without a tank. You didn't need a tank. You didn't need anything. You—" She backed up as he kept coming toward her, bumped up against the bridge. "That night in the lagoon. You kissed me. You breathed air into my lungs!"

It was too late to deny it.

"You don't have to be afraid of me, Sienna. I'm not going to hurt you."

"I am scared to death of you!" she screamed. "What are you?"

"Those men—" He glanced over his shoulder quickly, then back. "Those men are going to pull up beside us in a few minutes. I found what looks like a merchant ship down there. We're out having a little fun, that's all. You've got to calm down."

"Calm down?" she shouted again.

"Calm down," he said again, quietly. He was inches away from her but afraid to touch her, afraid she'd explode. "When I was a child, my parents were part of a humanitarian mission to the island of Valuatu. The Soviets were funding a takeover of the entire chain of islands, using Adal

Chaba. He wanted to retake the island he'd ruled for twenty years before U.S. forces freed it, and they wanted to build a Pacific base. They had a secret deal with Chaba to do the dirty work in exchange for a position of power in the new communist government they planned to set up. Chaba wiped out an entire village with a chemical bomb. In the end, the U.S. moved back in and the islands retained their sovereignty."

Sienna face hadn't changed. He had minutes, scarce minutes, before the other boat would be upon them.

"Why are you telling me this?" she demanded wildly.

"A lot of people died, including my parents. A lot of children died, too. Children like Peter." He fought past the clenched pain in his chest. "But not all of them. I survived. So did others. Some of us had strange aftereffects from the blast, physiological mutations."

She blinked, and he could see her swallow. He took a chance and reached out to her. Touched her cold, damp cheek. Just that barest skim of his finger against her face and he could feel the shivering of her entire body.

"I don't need air the same way you do. My body processes oxygen through the water." He didn't need to explain everything else. It was too complicated, and there wasn't time. And there were too many things he couldn't tell her at all.

"I'm still a man, Sienna. I'm human, just like you."

A shout broke through the sound of waves and wind.

Sienna's eyes didn't move, didn't budge from his. Frightened.

"Hey, Brock! What's up?"

Luckily he'd come out of the water, up the ladder, on the other side of the boat. They wouldn't have seen him get out, noticed he had no gear. But Sienna—

He grabbed her hand, held on tightly when she would have ripped it away. He didn't know what she'd do. Try to run, beg for help. She'd looked at him as if he were a monster.

What are you?

Ripples of dark memory soaked. Old rejection, his friend again.

"Hey, Bo, Matt." The smaller boat slid closer. "Just doing a little diving. Just scrap down there, nothing too interesting. What's up with the rifles?"

Bo had a beer, no shirt, his lanky form burned brown in the sun. He was a dive junkie, a treasure hound. Matt was his brother, and Cade had crewed with them a few times. They couldn't keep their mouths shut to save their lives, which was why he'd stopped working with them. He'd lost a wreck or three to other hunters because of them.

"They found a couple dead in their boat this morning off Round Rock Island," Matt told him. He pushed the shaggy hair back that wind whipped in his eyes. "Just feeling weird today. They don't know who did it or why."

One of the shallow sites Sienna had marked was off Round Rock Island. Cade had a bad feeling he knew what had happened to the couple. They'd been in the wrong place at the wrong time. Chaba's men were already searching.

The boat rocked alongside now and Bo put down his beer, shaded his eyes.

"Tabitha Donovan!"

"She's not Tabitha." He held on, a surge of protectiveness rising. He didn't think Matt or Bo meant any harm to Tabitha. They'd been acquaintances, as far as he knew. Nothing more than that.

But they could do harm to Sienna, even without meaning to. Her hair was wet, her face was still bruised, but she was the spitting image of Sabrina, there was no way around it.

"You know Sab—Tabitha?" Sienna asked.

"Hell, yeah." Bo squinted. "Damn, you look exactly like her."

"Have you seen her? Recently? I'm looking for her."

"Are you her twin sister or something?" Matt asked.

"Have you seen her?" Sienna repeated.

Bo shook his head. "We haven't seen her in weeks."

"If you do," Cade put in, "don't tell her anyone's looking for her. Just tell me." He leveled his gaze on both the men and appealed to greed. "There'll be something in it for you."

Matt grinned. "Sure."

"We're heading back," Cade said. He reached for Sienna again. "Storm's coming up. You should be heading in, too."

"Just about to." Bo picked his beer up again. "You damn sure do look like Tabitha Donovan."

The two men were still drinking, their boat rocking with the waves, as Cade started up his cruiser and speeded back toward Little Eden.

If that helicopter flyover hadn't given Sienna away, Matt and Bo could. He was running out of time. He slid his hand under the bridge, took out the remote security device and checked the island for intrusion. None of the sensors showed disturbance. They would be safe tonight. The storm would shelter the island from attack.

First thing in the morning, he had to get Sienna out of there and turn her over to a PAX safe house. He'd call Beck and get a PAX team out to

Little Eden to begin a search in earnest. The murder off Round Rock Island meant Chaba's men were here, and Chaba would be, too. The terrorist leader wouldn't risk the globe in the hands of his henchmen. He'd want to be on-site when it was recovered. And Sienna... She knew too much, and not enough. He had to keep it that way.

And he had to keep himself sane, even if that meant saying goodbye.

The house was dark. Again, Sienna watched Cade operate a complex array of sensors before they could get inside the villa. He'd carried the rifle in with him from the boat.

Sienna stood there on the polished wood floor, still wet, cold and scared.

Alone on this island with this strange man who could breathe underwater. She hadn't imagined what had happened in that lagoon. It had been real.

He was real.

I'm still a man.

She didn't know what to think. She was exhausted, drained emotionally from the fear and panic and sheer physical stress of everything that had happened.

She'd gone diving. That alone still had her knees shaking.

And Cade… She didn't even know where to begin in processing what she'd discovered about him.

He set the rifle down on the granite counter in the shadowed kitchen. He hadn't said more than seven words to her on the way back to Little Eden. Now, he lifted his deep blue gaze, shuttered and dark.

Outside, the storm grew wild.

"I thought you were dead," she whispered. "When I found your gear…" Her throat contracted. But he hadn't been dead.

He'd been eighty feet down without an air tank.

Her life had been taken over by the unbelievable. From the moment she'd stepped out of the rental car in front of Sabrina's apartment in Key Mango, nothing had been the same. That Cade possessed some sort of fantastic physiology wasn't much less hard to swallow than the notion that terrorists wanted to kidnap her for the ancient secrets of the *Santa Josefa*, was it?

She closed the distance between them, reached out and touched the warm skin of his neck, trailed the thin bump of scar she could feel.

"You can…die, can't you?" she added in a whisper.

He wasn't magic. He was real. He was a man. She could feel his heat, his pulse, see his pain.

That sexy quirk of his mouth was visible even through the gloom. "I'm not immortal, Sienna."

The bitter twist to his low voice wasn't lost on her. Her heart wrenched. He wasn't immortal, but he was alone. Very alone. Here, on Little Eden, with his treasures and the sea.

"This is why—" She dropped her touch from him, waved her arm around the darkened space. "All of this. It's where you hide your secret."

He didn't answer.

She remembered that article she'd read about him. The rumors, the thinly veiled accusations. "I read a magazine piece at Sabrina's. Your name was in it, and your picture. That's how I knew about you. People think you're a thief, a renegade—"

"People have to have an explanation for why I find things other hunters don't find," he said shortly. "I don't steal. I don't take treasure that's not lawfully mine to take."

"And I guess if I told anyone you were some kind of…merman, I guess that would just add to your reputation," she said, a wave of disbelief washing over her again.

He stared at her for a long beat. He didn't answer.

"What happened after the bombing? You said you lost your parents."

"I was adopted."

"Then what?"

"They gave me back."

Gave you back? She didn't realize until she saw the stark light of his eyes that she'd said it out loud. "What kind of people give a child back?"

"I don't blame them," he said, yet she heard that bitter thread in his voice again. His gaze on her was steady, shuttered again as if he was well practiced in the art. "They wanted to help me. I was raised in…a clinic," he explained. "I was able to receive therapy there that made it possible for me to learn to live with my mutation. There were other children from Valuatu there, children with other abnormalities, and it was for the best."

She didn't agree with that statement. He'd lost his parents. She knew how painful that was. He'd lost his parents *twice.*

Now she understood. All the contradictions of him fell into place. He only seemed to be this playboy with his private island and his toys. His so-called hundreds of women.

His voice was low. "You can run away screaming now."

"I'm not afraid of you." And she wasn't. An odd peace settled over her even as the world outside spun into a raging storm that shook the house. There was a storm in his eyes, too. He looked almost afraid of *her.* "You accused me of fearing you. But maybe it's you who's scared of me." She wouldn't let his gaze go, held it. "Maybe you're scared I'm *not* going to run away."

"Silly girl. Run."

His dangerous voice hummed through her veins. "No."

"First thing in the morning, when this storm clears, I'm taking you off the island," he said. "I've got friends. A safe house. You can stay there until this thing is settled."

This thing. Sabrina. The *Santa Josefa*.

"I don't want to go." God, just this morning she'd demanded she'd only stay a few days, but now... She didn't want to leave. She wanted to find Sabrina. She wanted to find the *Santa Josefa* and the globe, and maybe now she had the key. "I think I remembered something."

He froze, and she went on in a burst. "There was another team of hunters after us that summer." More, even more than she expected, tore out. "My mother was drunk one night and she told someone we'd found the *Santa Josefa*." Agony seared her. Her mother had driven down that off-ramp on purpose, blaming herself for what had happened to her husband. Oh, God. Or that's what she'd thought, then she'd shut down.

The memories had started to come back after she got out of the hospital, but she'd shut down because she couldn't handle them. She wasn't sure she could handle them now. But she couldn't lose Sabrina, too. Her heart pounded painfully in her chest.

"What else do you remember?" Cade closed the space between them, grabbed her by the shoulders. His steady gaze seared her.

"I don't know! I— They found us. They must have found us. My father had some kind of plan. But I remember them coming at us with spearguns underwater. My father was hit."

A black hole of danger and fear threatened to swallow her. "Maybe that's what attracted the shark," she cried. "I don't remember what happened after that! But if I'm here longer, maybe it will come back." She just knew she couldn't go, didn't want to go. Not now. No matter how much it might hurt to stay. "We can't give up now."

Sabrina was still out there. Sabrina, and the truth.

Cade's face took on a grim, unreadable cast. "There's no we. Me."

Anger shot up inside her. "Since when do you think you can order me around? I have a mind and a will of my own."

"Then use some sense. This is no place for you. Did you hear what Matt and Bo said? They found a couple dead in their boat off Round Rock Island. Do you think it's a coincidence? They were in the wrong place at the wrong time. They got in the way of the wrong people."

Sienna's heart thumped. She'd been so stunned, still, from what she'd learned about Cade that she hadn't even connected those dots. Hadn't had time to think about it.

"And now Matt and Bo have seen you," Cade went on. "You look like Tabitha Donovan. If they spread that around—and trust me, they might, despite my offer—then you're in even more danger."

"You wanted me to come here. You wanted me to help. Unless you're going to tie me up and carry me on your back to that helicopter, you can't force me to leave. I don't want to be shuttled off to some friend of yours. This is my fight, too. Not just yours. I lost my parents because of that wreck, and I'm not going to lose Sabrina, too."

The deadly weight of the silence inside the house was broken by the beep of the satellite phone on the kitchen counter.

Chapter 13

Cade flipped on the kitchen light as he reached for the phone, recognizing the code in the display.

"Brock here."

"It's about Sabrina Parker."

He turned, met Sienna's wide gaze.

"Talk to me."

"She's dead."

He felt as if he'd been punched in the gut. He didn't give a flip about Sabrina Parker, the Tabitha Donovan he'd known. He'd seen her face when those men had come out of nowhere to attack him. She'd set him up. She'd smiled like a pleased cat. She'd walked away.

And she'd set up Sienna as a decoy at her apartment in Key Mango, not caring what happened to her own twin.

He cared about Sienna, though. He'd been readying himself for Sienna to find out that her sister was in this thing up to her eyeballs, intentionally, and that she'd used Sienna like a pawn in her evil game. But he hadn't steeled himself for this.

Sienna's eyes searched him now.

"What is it?" she whispered.

"Details," he spoke into the phone.

The agent relayed the information quickly, concisely, bringing Cade up to date on as much as they had at this point. He clicked off when he was finished and set the phone down.

There was no sound in the house but the slap of palm trees blowing against the house, the thunder of his heartbeat, the insistent beat of rain on the roof.

His chest ached with the words he had to say. Sienna stared up at him, her hair stringing damply against her cheek, her damp clothes sticking to her slim body, stress tensing her face.

He knew the emotional devastation he was about to inflict. As bad as it had been to think of her realizing Sabrina's perfidy, this was worse. Sienna would blame herself, and never see that Sabrina had been beyond her help all along.

"What is it? Something's wrong." She shivered

now as she stood there, though the house wasn't cold. Her face was pale, the streak of blue bruising still evident on one cheek.

She'd been through far too much in little more than twenty-four hours.

"Come sit down." He took her arm, pulled her into the living area. She resisted, stopping halfway.

"I don't want to sit down. I want you to tell me what's going on." She rooted her feet and he knew she wouldn't budge unless he used brute force. He released his hold.

"In the morning," he began carefully, "as soon as it's clear, we're going back to Marathon." Before she could protest, he went on. "That was a friend of mine…" He had to massage the facts here, lie to her again. "A friend in the police department. I asked him to keep an eye out for me regarding any information about Tabitha Donovan."

She moved her hand impatiently, not interested in how he got the information, just wanting it, now. "Where's Sabrina? Is she all right?"

"No, she's not all right, Sienna," he said as gently as he could.

She didn't move for a long moment, maybe didn't even breathe. "What do you mean?"

"They found a body today, washed up on the beach in Key Mango. The body of a woman."

The sharp intake of Sienna's breath tore

through his heart. Her huge, hurt eyes seared him. She backed up a step, as if she suddenly didn't want to hear any more. But she had to.

"The identification isn't complete, I want you to know that," he went on. "But she had a wallet on her. They don't think she'd been in the water very long. There were credit cards, driver's licenses, in both Sabrina Parker's and Tabitha Donovan's names. The physical description is a match." He stepped toward her, wanting to do something, needing to put his arms around her despite the equal need to keep his distance.

"But if the identification isn't complete, then maybe it's not her," she breathed brokenly. "It might not be her."

"They're going to want you to identify the body."

Sienna had to leave Little Eden now, despite her protests. And he should have been relieved, but not under these circumstances.

"You thought she set you up. You thought she set me up. I don't think any of that is true, and I don't think she's dead either." She sounded wild suddenly, and he knew this was her longing to believe anything but the truth, especially that her twin could be dead.

He nodded, locked with her haunting, aching gaze. "Maybe it's not her."

"If it is her…" Her words came out thick, agonized. "Then I was too late to do anything." Her voice rose. "I should have stayed there. She was in Key Mango. Maybe she went back to the apartment and they found her, killed her, threw her body in the water."

"You couldn't have done anything." He strode toward her, closed the gap and gripped her arms. "You couldn't have saved her."

"How do you know?" she cried.

"Because it would be you in that morgue right now if you hadn't gotten out of Key Mango!" he told her grimly. "Your sister was in trouble. A lot of trouble. And none of it was your fault or your responsibility." God, she was shaking like a leaf now, shock setting in. "You've got to sit down, Sienna."

"No, I don't want to sit down." She tore away from him. "I want to go back to Marathon now. I want to see the body."

"You know we can't go back tonight in this storm."

He could see the terrible struggle inside her as she faced that fact. She was out of her mind with grief and she was clinging to every shred of hope, but she was fighting a losing battle. She knew the type of men her sister had been mixed up with. She'd tangled with them herself. She knew two people had been found dead off Round Rock Island, and what that meant.

"Maybe if I hadn't been— Maybe if I'd faced all of this before— Maybe Sabrina would have been able to talk to me. Maybe I would have known what was going on and I could have changed something. Now— Now it could be too late."

"You can't blame yourself. It won't help her now."

"What will help her now?" she asked bleakly. "If that woman is Sabrina—" She bit her lip and squeezed her eyes for an awful second, then lifted them to him again. "How did she die? How did the woman die?"

He understood her need to know everything, but he hated the guilt laced through her question. He wanted to take that guilt away from her, and he couldn't. Even he didn't have all the facts about Sabrina's involvement with the terrorist plot. But he could tell her what the agent had told him about the body they'd found on the beach in Key Mango.

"They think she was probably dropped off a boat, not far offshore. Indications were she hadn't been dead more than six hours. She had shoulder-length blond hair, brown eyes, about your height and weight. They estimate she was about thirty years old." The description fit Sienna to a T. And therefore it fit Sabrina. His chest banded with the weight of his final words. "She'd been strangled."

The silence in the house was almost deafening. The storm seemed far away suddenly. All he could hear was Sienna's heart beating, hard.

"This isn't your fault, Sienna."

The dark shine of despair in her eyes all but choked him.

"I still don't want to believe it's her."

"I know." He wanted to comfort her, but he didn't know how. He could tell her to sleep, but he doubted she could do that. "We'll go to Marathon in the morning. I'm not going to let anything happen to you, Sienna."

Her gaze rose, grief-stricken. "Something's already happened to me," she whispered starkly.

The shower was hot and strong, and she stood in it for as long as she could. *She hadn't been dead more than six hours. She'd been strangled.*

She stood there, wishing she could cry. But if she did, that might mean she believed Sabrina was dead. And she couldn't let herself believe that. Her eyes burned and her chest ached as she got out of the shower, dressed in a plain peach T-shirt and jeans.

The bed that had looked so inviting that morning looked like hell now. She'd never sleep. Grief and fear threatened to consume her whole and somehow, some way, she had to focus on hope or she'd go crazy tonight.

She found Cade in the kitchen. He pushed a bowl of soup across the granite counter. She took a seat on a stool at the bar and wondered how the hell he thought she could eat. He poured her a glass of wine and set it in front of her.

"Are you trying to get me drunk?" A sob choked her throat and a new curl of guilt streaked through her. Her sister could be dead and she was making a stupid crack.

"The wine might help you sleep," he said quietly.

There was concern in his eyes, and it was almost more than she could take. She didn't want sympathy. Sympathy meant Sabrina was dead.

"I need to do something," she said. She pushed the soup away. "I really appreciate this. It was thoughtful. But I can't eat."

She took the wine and the bowl and carried them to the sink. She needed to be busy, distracted.

He nodded. "All right," he said. "I understand."

A few minutes later, he sat down behind the desk in his study and turned on the computer. Sienna sat across from him, watching. He picked something up off the desk, a small chip, and he pushed it into a drive attached to the computer. Images appeared on the screen, and she realized this was the video from the boat. He studied the murky imagery, tracking the pattern of the scrap on the seafloor, then went back to study the shape of the hull sticking out of the sand again.

He kept staring at it, stopping the images, clicking through to zoom on one after another. The concentrated look on his face left her wondering what he was thinking and not telling her.

"Tell me about these men you remember."

She shook her head. "I can't remember anything else. It doesn't make sense to me now. My father was killed by a shark attack. I was attacked by a shark. I know this. I don't know what I'm remembering about these other men. Maybe I'm wrong. I've never had more than disconnected memories of that summer."

She watched as Cade clicked through to newspaper archives from the keys.

"What are you looking for?" she asked, moving around the desk to perch on the edge of it, get closer.

"Proof that you're right." The clock ticked on the other side of the room as the storm beat outside.

He stopped scrolling and leaned into the screen.

Two bodies, badly decomposed, had washed up on Piney Point fifteen years ago, in the winter. Reports suggested they'd been the victims of a shark attack and the men had remained unidentified.

"There are your two men," he said. "The date

fits with the time you and your father were attacked, given time for them to wash ashore."

Sienna wanted to be excited, but hope was still far away. And she didn't know what to make of the men with spearguns being involved on the day of the attack.

Cade looked up at her.

"Piney Point's directly in line with the last site we searched today."

"But you said there was just junk at that site."

His edgy dark gaze connected with her. "I don't know what that means yet, but I'm going back."

She swallowed tightly. Back without her, that's what he meant.

"I want to help. I *need* to help. For Sabrina."

He shook his head. "I can't let you." He reached out, put his hand over hers where it lay on the desk beside her. "A lot of lives are at stake, Sienna. If this is it, if I can find the globe, maybe hundreds of thousands of lives can be saved by keeping it out of the hands of terrorists."

He was telling her that even if Sabrina died, even if she couldn't do anything more, she hadn't failed if he found the globe because of her. And he—

"You're not doing this just to add to your private collection, are you?"

His face was unreadable, hard. She didn't buy

any of this carefree playboy act of his. He might have made his money off the treasures of the sea—but she didn't believe anymore that he was some kind of unscrupulous renegade.

"You were the victim of a terror attack," she went on. "You're doing this to save lives, not because you want the globe."

"Don't start turning me into a hero, Sienna." His voice was low, fearsome suddenly. "I'm not one."

"What are you, really?" she asked. He'd lied to her from the beginning, but for every truth she uncovered, there seemed to be more buried.

His face remained carefully guarded. "You don't want to know."

She'd given all her truths to him, and he wasn't about to give anything back. She felt angry, and stupidly hurt.

"I still want to come back," she told him. "I want to come back here with you tomorrow after—" If that body was Sabrina's… There was nothing she could do but fight to make sure her sister was the last one to die. And if it wasn't, then she could still make a difference, still save her. She could help Cade find the globe.

He stood, and the study shrank to him and her.

"I don't need you anymore, Sienna. You're not coming back."

"You don't *need* me?" She reached out and

poked his powerful chest. He'd showered and changed, too, and he smelled like soap and man and darkness that pulled her beyond comprehension. Suddenly, she knew this was about more than the *Santa Josefa*. More than the danger. "Why are you so eager to get rid of me?"

"I want you safe, and there's nothing more you can do."

"That's not true. Oh, I believe you want to keep me safe, I do. But I think you're keeping yourself safe, too. You knew you were putting me in danger when you took me here today. That didn't stop you. But now—" She canted her head, studied him. "When we kiss—" She couldn't even think of the words to describe what happened when they kissed.

And even now, so close to him, she felt that awareness, that energy, crackle between them like a living, breathing creature.

"Kiss me again," she demanded, then added, "I dare you."

She saw his eyes flick to her mouth, inches away from his. Her heart pounded as his hot gaze rose to hers.

"If I kiss you again," he admitted, low, "it's not going to stop there."

"Maybe I don't want it to."

"Stop it, Sienna." His voice was rough, bitter

in warning. "You aren't the kind of woman who has one-night stands. And I am not the kind of man who has anything else."

Wind shook the house again. Rain beat down outside.

She tilted her chin up just a bit.

"I don't think I'm in love with you, if that's what you're worried about." She was in love with the mystery of him, in love with the knowledge that he freed something inside her.

Something had happened to her out here on Little Eden. And he was part of it. She didn't want to walk away from that, or from him.

Whether it could turn into something else, she didn't know, and neither could he. That was part of the mystery, and while she was okay with that, she had no idea how to convince him. She didn't care about the danger, emotional or physical.

She'd started something here, both with Cade and the *Santa Josefa,* and she was in it for the finish, on both counts.

"I just want you," she whispered, "to kiss me again."

Chapter 14

Her blunt invitation sparked a wave of need he'd been keeping banked all day. Sienna stared up at him, so near, so desirable, her incredible amber eyes wide and serious. Then she lifted her mouth, a scant breath away, then closer.

Cade closed his eyes, reeling with hunger as she touched her mouth to his. Her tongue lightly outlined his lips then slipped inside. He groaned, need rocking through him. He deepened the kiss, filling his hands with the sweetness of her body, stunned by the almost violent ache in his heart.

I don't think I'm in love with you, if that's what you're worried about.

He'd lied to her again, lied that he didn't need her. Worse than that, he was afraid, bone-deep, that *he* could love *her*. And that would be a huge mistake.

"Sienna." He pulled his mouth away from hers. He could feel the full roundness of her breasts crushed against him.

Her expression didn't waver, as she said, "I want to make love with you. I don't care if it's just for one night. When I met you, I was scared. I've been scared for fifteen years, not just of the past, of the water, but of men, of sex, of feeling anything. I don't want to be scared anymore, Cade. I don't want to hide in my safe little library and watch life pass me by. This is life, you and me. Tonight. Whatever this is, I want to finish it."

She was impossibly beautiful, impossibly sexy, impossibly offering herself to him.

Something clenched again in Cade's chest. They didn't belong together. Sienna was here now, but no matter what she said, she'd be going back to that safe little library. She'd taken every challenge that had come her way between Key Mango and Little Eden—and she'd not only survived, she'd conquered. But she was only part of his world on a temporary basis, and that was how it had to be. He would hurt her in the end, and yet right now, she wanted him to make love to her.

After tomorrow, he'd never see her again. And if that thought hurt, he would deal with it later.

"You should go," he told her, "before it's too late." Before he ripped off her clothes and slammed her down on the desk. Before he took everything she was offering and more.

He didn't have to rip off her clothes. She pulled back and before he realized what she was going to do, she tore her shirt over her head. There was no bra. He would barely have to move his hand and he could cup her ripe breasts, barely tip his head to taste the tip of her nipple. She could have no idea of the hunger ripping and roaring through him. Then she reached for the button of her jeans and lowered her zipper. The soft slide of the material down her thighs pounded in his ears. Then she kicked them away.

The beat of the storm outside couldn't outmatch his pulse. Sweet God, she was standing in front of him naked. He knew the pull deep between his legs, the physical ache for her that was so much simpler to deal with than emotion.

"Sienna, you don't know what you're doing."

"Then maybe you need to explain it to me. In detail."

All the wanting, all the guilt, all the loneliness spun together and he kissed her. He had to kiss her, or he was sure he would explode. He pulled her into his arms, and nothing else existed. Not PAX. Not the *Santa Josefa*. Not the armed men waiting to wipe out the eastern seaboard. And sure as hell not his determination to avoid this very thing.

He swept his hands to the tight, sweet rounding of her bottom, lifting her up and onto the desk, and lowered his mouth to lick all the way down her neck. The sexy, natural scent of her filled his senses as he buried his face between her breasts. She fisted his hair as he took one hard, waiting nipple into his mouth. He tugged and sucked, her throaty whimpers driving him mad. She cupped the back of his head with her hand, driving him lower.

Pulling his head up, he met her aching gaze.

"Please don't tell me you're going to stop."

As if he could. He'd probably die.

Then she knocked him breathless by taking his hand and placing it there, between her thighs. His mouth crashed down on hers again even as he slid one finger, then two, higher, into her moist heat. She shuddered, and he nearly came undone right there. She grabbed his face, kissed his eyelids, his nose, his cheek, and that was it for him, he couldn't have turned back if someone had been holding a gun to his head. But she wasn't. She was begging against his mouth for him to take her. *Now. Hard. Fast.*

Charts slid, papers flew, a cup of pens rolled and

thudded on the floor. He pushed her back on the desk and she pulled him down with her. Heavy, sexily lidded eyes slashed to his for one hot beat of desperate connection he wasn't sure he'd ever understand. He started with her thighs, tonguing a line from her knee up, taking tender time at the scars, then licking his way down the soft inside of her other thigh till he returned to the burning center. He replaced his fingers with his tongue, spreading the creases of her sweet heat apart to enter deeper, pull on the little nub of pleasure inside, tasting her sex and her need. She cried out when he swirled his tongue around it then sucked hard again, her fingers clawing into his hair.

She was shivering as if she were cold, but he knew it was just the opposite. She was on fire, her hips rising up off the desk, pleading as he kept circling, flicking, pulling on the tiny bud of swollen need inside her. And he couldn't get enough of her, would gladly die this way, his mouth filled with her surrender.

Her fingernails dug into his shoulders as she fell apart, writhing, and he didn't stop, drank her in through the gripping contractions that were so open, so free, so uninhibited, they blew his mind. Fever raced over his skin as he tore his mouth from her sweet center to look into her dazed eyes, and for the first time since he'd crossed paths with her, there were no lies, just complete and vulnerable honesty.

This was honest, this crackling, powerful need, and the dangerous surge of his own yet unsatisfied desire had sweat running down his back. Then it was her hands running down his back, reaching for the bottom of his shirt, ripping it over his head.

"Sienna, sweetheart, I want to take you to bed right now." He couldn't stop touching her, rubbing his hands down her shoulders, her arms, her waist, breathing in the musky smell of her that was driving him wild. His pulse hammered and he ached, fiercely.

"Not yet," she said.

Not yet. That meant they weren't done. It was as though she'd decided that if they only had tonight, then they were going to do everything. That thought touched his heart sharply, and he would have said something more, he wasn't sure what, maybe *please* or *thank you,* but he couldn't speak for the choking hunger in his throat when her hand cupped his straining need through his jeans. She pushed him back and he stumbled, hit the wall of the study as she lowered onto her knees, tore down his zipper and slipped off his jeans. He helped her, picked up one foot, then the other, and then she slammed him back against the wall again, hard, with one hand to his stomach. With the other, she took his hard shaft in her hand and slipped it into her mouth.

He looked down and saw the curve of her tongue,

nearly lost it right there. He wasn't going to last two seconds with the buildup of pure sexual energy pounding through him, and she didn't give him much chance. He waited a moment, not sure he had the strength to move then dragged her up and into his arms, her body so warm and bare in his hands.

"Now you're coming with me."

"I hope so," she said.

Cade's eyes flashed brightly and all Sienna cared about was that he wanted her as much as she wanted him, wasn't any more finished than she. It took him one second to get her out of his study, five more to get her down the darkened hall to the door of his bedroom. Another two to slide her to her feet in the slate-tiled bathroom, rain beating down above them on the skylights.

Sienna couldn't take her eyes off his body, taking in his rigid, muscled chest, his lean, taut stomach, lower, to his already hard again shaft. He reached past her, opened the door of the shower, and she stepped back into it. He followed, twisting on the hot spray of water then taking her shoulders in his hands. A moan fell from her as he crushed tiny kisses all over her face, trailing his tongue down her shoulders, a bar of soap appearing from somewhere into his hands that he slid all over her back, her buttocks, her legs, following with his hot lips. Then she stole the bar from him and took her turn.

When she reached his rigid core, the soap slid out of her fingers as she encircled him. She wanted him, again, and he wanted her. All her life, since the first time she'd ever had sex, she'd been prim and proper and oh-so-careful, none of this raw hunger and exploding passion that made her want Cade to nail her against the shower wall and take her right here. And there. And a few other places, too. Until she just couldn't move anymore.

"I need you inside me," she told him simply.

But he wasn't done driving her crazy. He washed her hair, kissed her feet, and licked her in places she couldn't see, and then he carefully, gently, dried her off, picked her up, laid her damp, shivering body on his bed.

For a long beat in the shadowed room, he stared down into her eyes, then kissed her again. She welcomed his hot possession, slid her hand up his smooth shoulders and clung to him. The storm raged outside, lightning stabbing random light through the sheer curtains, but here was a strange peace even as her veins thundered with anticipation.

He moved leisurely, kissing every part of her skin as if he loved just touching her, tasting her, licking his way from her breasts to her belly button until she was moaning in need and he was reaching for the tiny packet he'd brought with him. Later, she knew she might wonder what had come over her, but for tonight, his warm, giving arms were all that mattered. When his mouth took hers again, she reached between them to touch him, made him groan as she rolled the condom on, and then finally guided him inside her. Between the flashes of lightning and the flashes of raw naked hunger, there was no reality but the one in his bed.

She dug her fingernails into his back, gripping him tightly, her legs wrapped around him. *Now. Hard. Fast.* And yet he rocked against her with maddening slowness, his pace impossibly arousing and taunting, his lips swallowing her gasped *please* as she clawed at him. A burst of pleasure seized her, and she cried out against his mouth. Finally, finally, he put his hands under her and pulled her up into his arms to meet his thrusts, quicker. The dark fire consumed her until her whole world revolved around just this, their bodies, surging together, all life and hot desire. She tore at the sheet beside her and cried out for him, the stranger who was her lover. And she knew she was irrevocably changed.

It was her wild abandon that did Cade in. He stayed with her as she came down from her completion, sobbing in his arms. Guilt sliced through him as he understood how vulnerable this moment was for them both, physically and emotionally. He'd failed to keep any distance between them of any kind, failed to protect her in the most intimate way possible, because he'd been prepared for everything but this feeling of every cell in his body being anchored to her.

And even as he hated himself for not keeping his distance in the first place, he pulled her tighter. He couldn't stop, wouldn't stop, the fierce ache for her burning him up from the inside out. When he collapsed beside her, his own release spent, their legs still damply tangled, he knew nothing but blessed sleep.

The soothing, after-storm dawn crept through the drapes in Cade's bedroom. Beside her, the even breathing of the man she'd given herself to so freely last night was the only sound. Sienna moistened her suddenly dry lips and knew the remembered ache between her legs.

There was a digital clock on the bedside table. It read 6:00 a.m. The house was dead quiet, the storm gone. She had no idea what time it had been last night when they'd finally slept, but what she did know was that her time here on Little Eden was nearly over. And as much as she'd demanded boldly that he bring her back, she couldn't force him. She swallowed hard thinking of the task ahead, viewing the body in the morgue back in Marathon.

She still couldn't believe it was Sabrina. They were twins. Wouldn't she know if her twin was dead? And yet she had to admit, she'd always been one to dismiss any extrasensory bond between them. They'd been close as children, but more and more different as they'd matured. She didn't know what Sabrina was thinking or feeling—if she had, maybe she could have stopped her from whatever was her involvement in this terrible situation in the first place.

A curl of fear tightened in her stomach. What if Cade was right? What if Sabrina had tricked her, used her, set her up in Key Mango? What if Sabrina really was a willing participant in a terrorist plot? There was no way she could accept that, but what was the truth of Sabrina's involvement?

The questions twisted in her mind and she wished the night hadn't ended. Wished she could have lost herself in Cade's heat forever. He was just one more question, and that last night, when she hadn't even cared about the answer, shook her. She'd been free in his arms.

No inhibitions, no fears.

She'd told herself and him that she wasn't in love with him, but there was no denying that even in her narrow band of experience with men, she knew this was different, because just looking at him now made her heart contract. She wanted to convince herself that last night had been nothing but the result of so many emotions in the past few days, but that would be a lie. She'd been waiting for the man who would finally make her so comfortable, she could be herself. The man who, instead of being outside her comfort zone, *was* her comfort zone. And wouldn't the irony be outrageous if that man was Cade Brock.

She padded on silent feet from Cade's room to his study in search of her clothes and her sanity.

The evidence of her wantonness was all over the place. The desk was a mess. She picked up the charts and papers from the floor and put them back. Her jeans were on the floor.

Her T-shirt in the corner.

Her panties under the desk. Next to his clothes.

She knew a dizzying surge of very vivid memory and her stomach dipped. His hands around her waist, his mouth locked on hers, his heat claiming her... *It was just an incredible sexual experience, that's all, don't make it more.* She bent and picked up the clothes, wadding them in her arms. An amazingly incredible sexual experience. Maybe the best sex ever.

But it wasn't more than that and she'd be a fool if she thought otherwise.

She was a fool.

Her heart was involved, to the hilt. And the thought of never seeing him again hurt so bad, she couldn't see straight for a second. Yet she knew that nothing that had happened last night would change his determination to see her off Little Eden for good.

She pulled on her clothes quickly and sat down at the computer, tapped the screen on. She clicked on the icon to bring back up the video chip imagery he'd been studying the night before. The murky pictures filled the screen and she stared at them, moving the images slowly. She'd been right about the men coming after them with spearguns—or at least it was clearly possible since they'd found the report of two bodies that showed evidence of a shark attack. She remembered her mother admitting to their father that she'd told someone in a bar about the site they thought was the *Santa Josefa,* the men tracking them down on the sea, coming after them, ready to kill them for the treasure.

Nets of junk seared into Sienna's mind. Chills shook her. She couldn't take her eyes off the images.

"Oh, God," she breathed, and shock rushed through her. She was looking at the *Santa Josefa.* That hull sticking out of the sand was the *Santa Josefa!* They'd found gold disks like those that had been carried on the *La Lucia,* one of the *Santa Josefa*'s sister ships, the one that had picked up the survivors and had made it back to Spain. Her father was convinced it was the *Santa Josefa,* that he'd really found it. They'd contaminated the site to stave off others until they could get the money to rent deep-sea equipment. And they'd found the globe that day—but never brought it up. Then the men with spearguns had found them.

And then there had been all that blood.

Sienna's hand slammed to her mouth. She could feel her heart pounding so hard in her chest, it hurt.

They'd been at the site of the *Santa Josefa* yesterday.

She clicked over to the on-screen chart Cade had marked with the coordinates, hit print on site six, the site they'd been to last the day before. He could leave her in Marathon, but he couldn't make her stay there.

Getting up from the desk, she folded the paper into a small square and shoved it in her back pocket before heading down the hall. She stopped at the closed door to Cade's room. She looked down the hall to the door that led to the guest room, then—

Turned back and looked up the hall to the study.

She'd been in every room in the house, including Cade's room. There were no doors between the study and Cade's door. His bedroom was large, but not that large. And the study was rather small. It had been, in fact, downright intimate last night.

The two rooms, knowing them both as she did now, didn't fit together.

She went back up the hall and stood in the door of the study again. He always kept it locked. Why? The entire house was as secure as some kind of military compound. He didn't have to lock the study unless he didn't want her in there alone. But last night, he'd forgotten. Last night, he'd left the study with her in his arms.

Curiosity killed the cat. Hadn't he said that very thing to her yesterday when he'd caught her poking around the house? *Stick your hand in a dark hole, don't be surprised if you find something that hurts.*

What had he meant by that? And suddenly her legs weren't trembling beneath her just because of the horrific memories that had returned.

As she stood there, the silence of the house bearing down on her, she heard something beep. Soft, muted, distant…and yet, not distant at all.

She strode to the wall of shelves filled with books and maps and artifacts. The beeping sound intensified. The hair on the back of her neck prickled and her heart boomed in her ears. She reached out, her fingers shaking for no good reason, and slid them along the shelves, then pushed aside books, scattered maps. The glass jar of gold doubloons teetered and crashed to the floor, scattering treasure at her feet.

Her fingers scraped across something that moved, a lever, and then the entire wall of shelves began to move.

Chapter 15

A bang broke into Cade's sleep. A second later, he was bolt upright, gaze slamming immediately to the remote sensor on the wall by his bedroom door. It showed no intrusion to the property.

And then he realized that wasn't where the intrusion was occurring.

He took the hall in bounds and crashed back the half-open door of his study. The wall of shelves hung open. He didn't have time to damn himself for the lapse in judgment that had made him carry Sienna out of here in his arms last night and leave the study door unlocked.

It was already too late.

She spun, papers in her hand, her eyes huge. She said nothing, but he could almost hear the pounding thud of her anger. He stood rooted for a dark beat in his own guilt, in the pain stabbing him from her gaze. She looked sick, shaken. Betrayed. His heart bolted to the base of his throat.

"Sienna—"

"Who are you?" she demanded, striding to him to slam the papers at his chest.

The documents rustled as they dropped to the floor. He knew what they were without looking. Memos, scans, transcripts, documentation of the League's case against Tabitha Donovan.

"You aren't trying to help Sabrina." Bitterness wrapped her words. "And you never were. You're trying to put her in jail. You're working for some kind of government agency. Who are you working for?"

He forced calm into his voice when he didn't feel calm at all. "I can't tell you that."

"What, you don't have a handy lie for that one?" She hit his chest again where he blocked the opening. "Get out of my way. I don't want to hear any more of your lies, anyway."

He grabbed her arm. "Listen to me, Sienna." His voice didn't come out steady now. It came out raspy, hoarse. Desperate. He'd known he couldn't keep Sienna in his life forever. Known he had to lose her. Hell, he didn't know if he had a life, not for much longer.

But he hadn't wanted her to hate him when they said goodbye.

"You've got to be kidding."

"There are a lot of things I can't explain. But you're right. I work for a secret agency. A covert arm of the government that no one sees, no one knows about."

"Are they all...like you?" She didn't take her eyes off his face. "Do they all have special powers?"

He shook his head. "I'm not at liberty to discuss that. You don't know how much danger you're in already because of what you know about me. I'm taking you to a safe house. You'll be debriefed there, and—"

"I'm not going anywhere with you except off this island." She was furious, her chest rising and falling with angry breaths.

"You don't have a choice. I'm sorry." God, he was so sorry. "You don't understand."

"No, I don't understand." She tried to shake her wrist out of his grip and made a sound of frustration when he held it fast. "It was one thing to lie to me about wanting the globe for yourself," she bit out. "And everything else you've lied about. But it's another thing to convince me that I was saving my sister from prison, not helping you put her in it!"

"Your sister is helping terrorists who want to blow up the eastern seaboard, Sienna. We're talking thousands, hundreds of thousands, possibly even millions of lives at stake!"

"So you say! And all you do is lie!"

"This is the truth. You've seen the evidence yourself now—photographs, transcripts of intercepted phone calls, her secret bank account. Where do you think that money came from?"

Her pulse beat visibly. "I don't know, but none of that proves anything. Not to me. Maybe she was set up—" She sounded wild, and he knew she was lying to herself, too hurt and shaken to process what she'd seen.

"That was Sabrina herself speaking in those phone transcripts."

"I don't care! I don't believe it. There has to be some other explanation." She hit his chest with her other hand. "You slept with me all the while you were using me to trap my own sister." That last came out on a choked sob. Her eyes suddenly swam with tears she wouldn't let fall.

The knife of guilt stabbed his gut. He grabbed her other hand. "*That* was real." *That* had been too real. He'd made love to her. Truth told, he'd done more than that. Way more. He was damn near in love with her, and maybe the word *near* didn't even belong there. But she was better off not knowing that. He wished to God he didn't know that. All that mattered now was that he'd hurt her, and nothing he could say would change the ugly truth of what she was facing.

"Please stop lying to me." Her amber eyes blazed at him, still swimming with pain, her chin held high.

He took a deep breath. "If what happened last night was a lie, this would be a hell of a lot easier for both of us right now," he told her, and he was shocked by the break in his voice. "I would give anything to make it easier for you, but I can't." He'd been stupid, and he'd gotten his cover blown, and now she was hurt even more.

He released his hold on her then, let her go. He'd said too much, and not enough. Neither one of them was in any shape for a rational conversation.

"Everything will be cleared up when we get back to Marathon," he told her, fighting for his own lost calm. "You'll be escorted to see—" He hated to say what she already knew. She was hurting enough, too much. On top of everything, she would be expected to cooperate in identifying what could be her sister's body. "Then you'll be taken to a safe house. You'll be out of danger. That's all that matters."

"Oh, thank you for telling me what matters," she said snidely. "I wasn't sure."

He shook his head, the look on her face slowly killing him. "I never wanted things to turn out this way, Sienna." He reached for her and she flinched, hit the desk with her hip. "Goddammit, I'm not going to hurt you!"

"No, of course not." Her voice cracked. "You would never do that!"

She stood there, very still, for an awful moment. "I wish I'd never laid eyes on you. I was right about you in the beginning."

The sensor box on the wall beeped and lit a red dot charting intrusion on the beach. Cade strode past Sienna to the computer, tapped the mouse to bring up the screen.

"There's someone on the beach." He slammed the mouse, bringing up a zoom shot. A boat had been pulled alongside the dock in his cove, and a figure was crossing the sand toward the pergola. "It's Matt."

Sienna was off like a rocket through the house. She'd brought nothing here that belonged to her, and all she wanted was off this damn island. Away from Cade and his lies and the scraped bruising he'd made of her heart.

And when she left, she didn't want to be taken

hostage by this shadow agency of his. She had to get to the police. The real world. Sanity. And he wasn't going to stop her. She grabbed the rifle off the kitchen counter as she ran.

She barely felt the knob in her hand as she flung the French door in the kitchen wide and hit the pergola deck in her bare feet. Behind her, she could hear Cade coming. Her stomach, and her heart, jumped into her throat. Matt was safe and he had a boat. He was her only way out. She hit the sand, feet flying.

Matt stopped short, seeing her coming. Beyond, she could see the boat and Bo but her gaze ripped to Matt. She'd get off Little Eden, get back to Florida. She'd go to the police with everything. Secret agency, no secret agency. She didn't know what to believe, how much of what else Cade had told her was a lie.

And she had about two seconds to convince Matt to help her.

"Please take me away from here. He's holding me against my will. Sabrina's in trouble, and so am I." She grabbed his arm, tried to pull him. "I need your help!"

He didn't budge. "I know where Sabrina is."

Her mind skidded. "What?" She heard footsteps pounding on the deck behind her. "There's no time!"

"Sienna, run!"

Dammit, she was trying to run! *Away* from him!

She dragged on Matt's arm, frantic, blood rushing in her ears. "Help me—" The plea died in her throat. The other man coming toward her wasn't Bo. And there was a gun in his hand.

"Run!" Cade roared.

Bullets splattered the sand around her. Matt gave an awful *ooof* sound from his throat and she watched as in horrific slow motion he collapsed at her feet. She whirled to race back to the pergola, her brain running twenty steps ahead of her. Cade kept running—toward her. He took the deck stairs in two bounds, hit the sand.

"Get in the house, Sienna!"

She was aware of a shadow in the corner of her eyes, coming at her from the other side of the house.

"Drop the gun!" the man ordered and shots hit the sand at her feet.

The rifle fell out of her hands.

The man reached her first, slamming her back against a hard chest. Something jammed into her temple. Cade stopped short, a gun in his hand trained straight over her shoulder at the man holding her.

Her gaze slammed with Cade's.

"Let her go," he ordered.

Oh, God, it was just like in Key Mango. Only this time, they hadn't waited inside. They'd waited outside, used Matt as a decoy to get them out.

Matt was dead now.

Her legs felt numb and blood roared in her ears.

"Kill him," the man holding her said.

More horrific slow motion. Her gaze swung in surreal fear to the other man approaching across the beach, his gun aimed at Cade while Cade's weapon was aimed at the man holding her. A stand-off in which Cade could only lose.

A shot boomed. Sienna screamed as Cade rocked backward, hit the deck railing. Blood spurted from his shoulder.

"Cade!" she screamed.

I'm not immortal, Sienna.

She fought and the gun suddenly left her temple only to slam back against her head. Stars rocked her vision.

"What do you want?" she begged thinly, hanging on to consciousness, fighting for it. "Let him live, please. I'll give you whatever you want." Her heart ripped. He'd saved her life, over and over, and whatever she did now, she wasn't going to cost him his.

"She wants you to live," the man yelled at Cade, forcing Sienna forward. Her head swam. "Do you want her to live? Throw me your weapon."

Cade tossed the gun on the sand. Sienna felt tears stinging her cheeks. She hadn't even realized she was crying. His hot, glassy gaze held hers.

"Step back."

Cade stepped back. Blood seeped down his arm.

"Let her go," he demanded again, pain sharp in his voice. "She doesn't have what you want."

"Yes, I do!" Sienna cried. "Just don't hurt him. If you kill him, I'll tell you nothing."

She could barely see the man holding her. His brutal grip had her back hard against him. She could feel heat, cruelty, and she had no doubt he'd kill Cade, just like he'd killed Matt, and not even blink.

"I can give you what you want," she whispered painfully. "I can take you to the globe." She couldn't. Not if these were the terrorists Cade had told her about, and who else could they be? But she could get them to take her away from here. She could get them to leave Cade alive. Maybe his agency would come in time. She'd been ready to run for her life away from that shadow agency, but she would give anything now if they would just drop down out of the sky.

Because if they didn't drop down from the sky, if they didn't come in time, these men were going to kill her, later if not sooner. Just like Matt. But not Cade. Please, God, not Cade. He'd lied to her so many times, but always it had been to protect her from these very people. And she knew now he'd never lied to her about them.

The man's grip tightened and her heart boomed in her ears again. "Take care of him," he ordered the other man. "But don't kill him."

Sienna didn't know what he meant until in an awful blur the other man lifted his gun and fired a shot at Cade, hit him in the thigh. He rocked backward to the sand, and the man reached him, slashed down with his arm even as Cade struggled to stand, and crashed his pistol across his head.

When he fell this time, he didn't get back up.

She boarded Matt's boat at gunpoint. There was no sign of Bo. They pushed her onto the decking in the rear of the craft. Her arms were jerked up, her hands tied to the railing.

Her head throbbed and she tasted blood where she'd cut her lip when she'd fallen as they shoved her into the boat. Oh, God, Cade. Huge tears ran unchecked down her face. Shot, beaten, unconscious, was there even a chance he was going to live?

He'd lie there and bleed to death....

Her stomach rose in her throat again, nausea and pain almost doubling her over, only she couldn't double over. She couldn't move.

She didn't know how much time had passed when footsteps pounded on the decking toward her. She opened her eyes as the man who'd shot Matt untied her hands and yanked her to her feet, shooting new pain into her head. Black dots swam in her vision and she struggled to see. The boat had stopped, she realized as the deck rocked under her feet.

"Chaba's waiting for you."

Chapter 16

Consciousness seared through Cade in a blinding rush, hot pain ripping his shoulder apart, firing his thigh, shooting black ribbons through his vision.

"They killed him. They killed Matt."

Cade turned his head toward the voice, darkness swamping him, threatening to suck him under. He fought for awareness. Bo's face, streaked with tears and sand, wavered beside him.

"We were at the marina this morning in Key Mango," Bo said thickly. "It was still dark. We were just going to go out, do some fishing. Some guys were asking about Tabitha. I was talking to this chick who works the counter. I wasn't paying attention and when I looked around, Matt was gone. I went outside and saw one of those guys pushing him into the boat. I tried to get there, but I was too late. The boat pulled away."

"How'd you get here?" Cade struggled to get up using his good arm, realizing his shirt had been cut away. Bo had found the first-aid box in the kitchen and his shoulder was taped, blood seeping through. The leg of his jeans had been ripped up the sides, the wound there taped, too.

"I borrowed a boat from another guy," Bo told him raggedly, "and told him someone was stealing our boat. But I couldn't find them in the dark. After it got light, I thought maybe they were after that girl, the one who looked so much like Tabitha, so I came here. Matt must have told them about her. Now he's dead. He's on the beach, dead." Bo's red-rimmed eyes tore into him. "I should have been with him. I should have been there."

"Help me up." Cade grabbed Bo's arm. The shelving was opened, the way he'd left it when he'd crashed out of there. There were documents, things Bo didn't need to see in the study. Bo was so messed up, he probably hadn't even thought to look for the satellite phone, or if he had, he hadn't found it. But he'd stopped Cade from bleeding to death. He'd probably saved his life. Now he had a chance to save Sienna's and nothing was going to stop him. Fire ripped through him as he made it to his feet. "Did the bullet go through my shoulder?"

"Yeah. I think so. The leg, it's just a flesh wound. You were bleeding pretty bad, man." Bo's gaze was stark, his face white. "I couldn't do anything for Matt…" He sounded like he was about to break down.

Cade clenched his jaw, forced himself to start walking as if pain weren't exploding through him with every step. "I'm calling for help. Stay here. I'll be back."

He kept moving, kept focusing. He reached the study and shut the door, moved into the annex and grabbed the phone, trying like hell not to jostle his burning shoulder with every tiny movement. Hurting too much to see straight, he punched the code into the phone as it lay flat on the desk then picked it up.

"Brock here. Where's the team?" Thank God a team was already headed out to Little Eden. "We've got a change in plans."

Sweat dripped down his body by the time he locked up and went back to the living area, where Bo had practically collapsed on the sofa.

"Help's on the way," he told Bo tightly. "The house is secure. The windows are bulletproof.

Don't leave the house. Lock the door behind me."
Where was he going, Bo couldn't go. And even if
he could, Bo was in no shape to help.

"You can't go after them alone!"

"I can."

PAX choppers were on the way, but he wasn't
waiting. He had to get there first, and he had to get
there without them seeing him coming. There were
ten sites, and he had no idea what Sienna would
have told Chaba or even if she understood at this
point that they'd found the *Santa Josefa* yesterday.

All he knew was that if he didn't find her alive,
he didn't care if Chaba had the secret to saving his
own life. He'd be too busy killing him with his
bare hands to get it out of him. He'd told himself
he was ready to say goodbye to Sienna this morning, send her away with PAX, but that had been
just another lie.

He made it out of the house and down to the
cabin cruiser. Five miles out, he cut the engine, anchored, strapped on his speargun and programmed
the coordinates into his underwater GPS unit, then
clipped it along with his remote communicator to
his side, and dove in.

They transferred her to another boat after she'd
faced Chaba. It was larger, better-equipped, but
she didn't see much of it before they shoved her

down into the pitch-black below-deck compartment. The door above slammed shut.

Chaba's cruel face burned into her mind. He was a shockingly small man, old and thin and radiating evil. He wore a uniform as if he were still the military dictator of Valuatu Island. His henchmen snapped to his orders, and he expected her to do so as well.

He'd slapped her across the mouth when she'd hesitated.

Tell me what I want to hear, he'd demanded. *And it had better be the truth.*

She'd lied. No way could she point him to the *Santa Josefa.* He'd never find it, not with the contamination her father had lain on the seabed, not if he didn't *know* it was there. She'd die if Cade's agency didn't show up. But there were hundreds of thousands of people who could also die if that artifact truly held secrets that mapped the earth's tectonic plates, allowing Chaba to strike the eastern seaboard.

She closed her eyes, tasting the blood on her split lip as the boat roared, picking up speed, heading for the wrong destination. The dark closed around her, suffocating her in horror.

"Sienna?"

Her pulse rocked and her head jerked up, her eyes straining in shock through the barely penetrable dark. There was a slight crack of light coming through the door above and her eyes adjusted, stunned. A shadow, a form—

"Sabrina?"

Shock rooted her, then she crawled, tore toward the barely perceptible form.

"Sabrina!" Her hands raced over her sister's arm, to her shoulder, felt her face, her hair tangled and damp. "Oh, God. You're alive." Sobs choked her. "I thought you were dead. They told me you were dead. They found a body—"

"They found someone, killed her. Just because she looked like me." Sabrina's voice came out thick, slurred. "They knew people were looking for me. I don't know who…"

Sienna's mind raced. Cade's agency. Then Chaba had gotten wind that someone was looking for Tabitha Donovan and they'd planted Sabrina's ID on her and killed her. She felt sick. Sabrina was alive, but someone else had died. Just like those two people in the boat off Round Rock Island.

"They told me about finding you in Key Mango," Sabrina went on. "They found your identification in your bag and they knew it wasn't me. I'm so sorry. You could have been killed because of me. I'm sorry."

"All I care about is that you're not dead." Sienna reached in the dark to push the hair out of her sister's face. She could pick out the shine of Sabrina's eyes. "Are you all right?"

"They gave me something, some kind of drug." Sabrina sighed, and groaned. "All my fault." She started crying softly. "It's all…my fault."

Sienna stroked her hair, crying, too. She wanted to tell her it was going to be okay, but it wasn't. Sabrina was alive for now, but for how long would either of them stay alive?

"What happened?" she whispered desperately.

She heard Sabrina groan again as she tried to push up on her hands. She helped her sit up, lean against the wall of the cabin.

"Looking for someone to help me find the *Santa Josefa*. That's all." Her words came out slow, difficult. "I met a man."

"Who?"

"Said his name was Tony, but I found out later his name was Chaba. Adal Chaba. Heard I was looking for someone to finance the *Santa Josefa* search. So many sites. I needed help. I was scared of him. I don't know why, he was just so… I stopped answering his calls—"

"That's the man you were afraid of." Chaba. The man who'd blown up his home island, destroyed Cade's family. He'd been responsible for minor terror attacks targeted at U.S. tourists abroad in recent years, too, she knew from the news. But what he had planned now wasn't minor at all. "What about Cade?" She swallowed down the sob saying his name brought to her throat. "Cade Brock."

"Cade." Sabrina repeated his name slowly, as if working to understand what she was asking. She sounded as if she might fall unconscious any minute.

"Stay with me, sweetie," Sienna begged. If there was any chance in hell of getting out of here, she had to know exactly what she was into, everything Sabrina could tell her about these people and their plot. "Why did they try to kill Cade?"

"I was meeting him. Charts. Going to sell them to him."

"But you didn't."

"Couldn't make up my mind. Then Tony's men— Following me. They tried to kill him. I got away, but I was so scared. So scared." She moaned again.

"What happened then?"

"I hid out. Motel on Thunder Key. Had a line on this rich collector from New York. Supposed to meet him yesterday."

"What happened?"

"Followed him, they must have followed him. When I got to the restaurant, his car was in the lot and he was dead, shot through the head. Before I could run… Grabbed me."

Oh, God, and what had they done to her?

"But why did you tell me to come?" Sienna asked. "Why did you tell me to meet you in Key Mango at your apartment?"

"I called you," Sabrina slurred. "Called and called. Told you not to come… Then they told me you were there, they saw you in Key Mango. Told me they were going to find you and kill you. They know you know where the *Santa Josefa* is. I'm sorry. Last night, they beat me." She started sobbing harder.

Sienna's heart tore. God, what had happened to her? The calls, she didn't get them. Why?

"It's okay." Her mind raced. Sabrina was almost incapacitated, but there were two of them now. If they could get one of Chaba's henchmen down here, alone, and if he thought she was Sabrina, maybe she could take him by surprise. Get his gun.

They'd have a chance of staying alive until Cade's agency, whoever they were, got here. If Cade had lived, if he'd gotten to a phone—

There were a million ifs, but it was all she had.

"I'm going to start screaming in a minute," she said. "I'm going to tell them I think you're dead. One of them will come down here, maybe, if we're lucky. I'll pretend to be you. What are you wearing?"

She ran her hands down Sabrina's side. Some kind of bike shorts and a tank top.

"Switch clothes with me. I'll lay down here, and God, Sabrina, you just have to be strong, for a few minutes. Sit up, pretend to be me! They know you're drugged. They won't be so careful around me if they think I'm you."

She was already ripping her shirt off, helping Sabrina pull hers over her head. In rapid movements, she did the same with her jeans and Sienna's shorts.

"They'll kill us," Sabrina slurred, fear laced through her voice.

"They're going to kill us anyway. And they're going to kill a hell of a lot of other people if they get the globe. I gave them the wrong coordinates. When they find out—"

"I can't do this."

She felt Sabrina sliding down the wall toward the floor.

"Yes, you can!"

"It was supposed to be ours. Daddy said it was ours. The *Santa Josefa* was going to change our lives."

"Sabrina!" She shook her sister's shoulders. She was slipping away into her fog and she needed her!

"I should have been with you guys that summer."

"You're lucky you weren't."

"They're going to kill us. Even if they find it, they're going to kill us," Sabrina moaned.

"You're not going to die if you'll just sit up and help me!"

"Where is it?" Sabrina whispered. "Promise I won't tell. I know they're going to kill us anyway."

Dammit! Sienna wanted to shake her again. She remembered how Sabrina had told Chaba whatever he'd wanted to know before.

"I can't tell you," she said. "Please, get up. It's our only chance."

"Don't make me do this," Sabrina sobbed and rolled over. "You always wanted to tell me what to do, do the right thing, have principles, play it safe."

God, what was she talking about?

"We have to—"

Sabrina rolled back and something small, glinting silver in the crack of light, appeared in her hand. "Tell me where the *Santa Josefa* is." Her voice was suddenly clear and hard and utterly lucid. "This is my game, and we're doing things my way." She pointed the gun at Sienna. "He's going to kill me if you don't tell me, just like he killed that guy last night."

"What are you doing?" Sienna choked out. Her head reeled.

"Tell me where the damn globe is!"

She wasn't drugged. She wasn't drugged at all. Sienna stumbled backward. "No, Sabrina—"

"Yes, Sabrina," Sabrina spat, advancing toward her, the gun never wavering in its bead on Sienna's chest.

Everything Cade had said about Sabrina was true. Horror rocked her.

"You're my sister," she whispered.

"That's right. And you've been keeping your damn secret for years. You knew where the *Santa Josefa* was all this time—"

"I didn't know! Not till today, this morning. Sabrina, people are going to die! They think that globe has evidence of the earth's original plate structure. They want to use it to set off tidal waves that could wipe out hundreds of thousands of lives on the eastern seaboard—"

"Then move west!" Sabrina screeched. "Now tell me where it is!"

"They'll kill you, too, don't you see?" Sienna pleaded desperately. "They're using you—"

A harsh laugh came out of Sabrina's throat. "I'm not an idiot, Sienna. I know at least two other collectors who are interested in the globe. God, there are probably plenty more. They can't shoot them all and no way am I handing it over to Chaba for free. Chaba beat the shit out of me last night, but this isn't over yet. I'll prove to him he can trust me when I tell him where it is." Her eyes glittered. "I'll get the globe then get away from him with it. He'll trust me after today."

"How the hell do you think you're going to do that? Chaba will find you, and he'll find the globe! Even if by some miracle you *do* get away with it, he'll go after whoever you sell it to, you know that! The globe has to be turned over to the authorities!"

"I don't give a rat's ass about the authorities! I want the money!"

She was insane. She had to be insane. She'd do anything for the money she could get from selling the globe, even at the cost of untold numbers of lives.

"You set me up at the apartment, didn't you?" she breathed in horror. There had been no phone messages…

The shadow form of Sabrina shrugged. "Whatever." She reached down with her free hand and pulled at the waistband of the pants. "Have you lost weight? These pants are killing me."

"You set Cade Brock up, too," Sienna breathed.

"He's a charmer, isn't he?" Sabrina's eyes narrowed. "You didn't fall for him, did you? He doesn't do relationships, sweetie. He's not for

Goody Two-shoes you. Besides, there's something wrong with him."

Sienna's heart thumped harder. "What do you mean?"

Sabrina shrugged. "I don't know. Chaba checked him out, after he caught me with him, found out his name. He told me Cade had a disease or something."

Did Chaba know the truth about Cade, the truth about what that Valuatu bombing had done to the survivors?

"What do you mean?"

"Something about some chemical blast. Apparently Cade was in some bombing attack Chaba was behind. He used some kind of secret chemical. Said it screwed up anyone who survived it. If they don't know the secret chemical— and no one does but Chaba—it'll kill them, eventually."

Oh, God. Cade and his no relationships rule. Was this his last secret? Hope shrank. Even if she made it out of this alive somehow, was Cade doomed?

"What's this?" Sabrina's hand slid into the pocket of Sienna's jeans. She pulled the folded sheet out. The paper cracked in the taut air as she slammed it open. "Oh, my God," she whispered. "Those freaking idiots. All they had to do was search you!" She laughed. "Now I'm the hero!"

Sienna's stomach dropped. Sabrina tilted the paper to the crack of light then she stepped backward quickly, shoved it in her pocket again and slammed her hand at something on the wall.

"Site six," she dictated. "The *Santa Josefa* is site six."

Oh, God. It had to be some kind of intercom, Sienna realized. And she'd just given the correct coordinates to the top.

Sabrina wheeled around, taking her hand off the button. "By the way, you don't think they'd really give me bullets." She laughed. "You're such a moron, Sienna." She turned back, hit the button again. "Hurry up! I'm waiting!"

There wasn't time to think, thank God, because it was almost impossible to do even without time. Sienna charged forward and slammed Sabrina's head into the wall.

Her sister dropped like a rock. The gun skidded across the floor.

The door of the below-deck compartment opened and light spilled. Footsteps pounded downward.

Sienna grabbed the empty gun. Sabrina's clothes. Sabrina's gun. They'd beaten Sabrina, so even their bruised and battered faces couldn't be much different.

"Get up top," the man ordered, waving her toward the steps with his gun. "Chaba wants you."

Chapter 17

Cade came up out of the water silent, deadly. It would only take him one shot to pick off Chaba's henchman pacing the deck, but the gun only held one spear and he wasn't wasting it yet. Instead, he slipped along the hull of the boat and crawled halfway up the dive ladder, waiting for the guard to come closer.

He shot over the side of the boat as the man passed and wrapped his arm around his neck, cracking it as he pulled him over. The body splashed into the water, and he waited, breath held, to see if anyone heard. The bandages were long gone and he'd just as long ago become numb to anything other than the driving need to get what he came for.

There was music coming from the forward compartment. Classical music, played loud, thank God. As he slipped over the side of the boat, he could see through the plate glass rear of the compartment to the man he'd been waiting most of a lifetime to kill.

Chaba. Smoking a cigar, feet propped on the bridge, listening to music, waiting for the divers Cade knew had to be below somewhere. He wasn't interested in Chaba's divers, not now. He wanted Sienna, and he wanted the truth out of Chaba. The divers down below were never going to get out of here with the globe. PAX would see to that.

He unclipped the remote communicator, punched in the code then the number six. PAX choppers would already be on the way, and now they'd know which site to zero in on. There were no signs of life on the boat. As he'd suspected, Chaba had come himself for the artifact, bringing only a few of his henchmen along.

Steps and a door led to a below-deck compartment. On soundless feet, Cade crept to the door, pulled it open. Light flared inward, touching the peach of Sienna's shirt. She lay so still, deadly still, her blond hair tangled around her face.

His heart almost exploded in his chest when her head moved and she moaned. The need to go to her, hold her, nearly devastated him. But he had to settle for knowing she was alive.

That meant it was him and Chaba now.

Quietly, carefully, he lowered the door. He had mere minutes before PAX would arrive now that they had the correct coordinates.

He crept, bent, to the doorway of the forward compartment then rose in one swift move, coming through the opening. "Hands up," he yelled over the music.

Chaba jolted in his seat, knocking the radio off the console as he jerked down his feet. The cigar he'd held in one hand went flying. The radio crashed to the deck and suddenly nothing but waves and pounding heartbeats sounded in Cade's ears as he faced the man he'd hated most of his life. He was shrunken, hardly the sturdy military figure he'd seen in old pictures, his hollow cheeks blanching as he swung around. Chaba started to dive for an Uzi on the bridge, but stopped at the click of the spear in Cade's gun as he punched it to the Fire position.

"I wouldn't reach for that if I were you," Cade said grimly. "Because there's nothing I'd like to do more than put this arrow right between your eyes to avenge my parents, my brother, and every other soul you took out on Valuatu Island."

"Cade Brock." The terror leader's eyes glittered, glassy, and Cade could see the stunned confusion he controlled even as Chaba's gaze darted around the boat. Looking for the henchman Cade had already killed, wondering how the hell he had shown up out of nowhere, with no warning.

The high-tech luxury cruiser rivaled Cade's own for its equipment and amenities, including a monitor that showed a constant greenish night-vision image of the dark below-deck compartment where he could see Sienna, still on the floor.

"You must be wondering how I got here, since your men left me to bleed to death on Little Eden." Cade kept the spear trained between Chaba's eyes. "I'm not planning to answer that question, but you're going to answer one for me."

The terror leader's brutal gaze sharpened in his shrunken face. The hand itching to grab that Uzi and blow Cade's head off clenched and unclenched.

"You know damn well there's a kill order on you, Chaba," Cade went on. "U.S. government choppers are on the way here right now. They can either find you dead, or they can find you alive. It all depends on how you answer the next question. What was in those bombs you used on Valuatu Island?" Cade's finger curved over the firing mechanism. "It's your only chance to see tomorrow, Chaba. Do you want to die? It's not going to be pretty, or painless. And the truth is, you're a coward, aren't you? You have no trouble killing thousands of people from a distance, though, do you? It's man to man now."

Chaba's gaze narrowed. He rocked slightly as waves lapped the boat. "I don't think so. What about your pretty lady friend, Brock? You want her to die, too? My diver already has his orders. She's not coming back up. I guess you can waste that spear on me, or you can try to save her."

"She's in the below-deck compartment. And she's alive."

"You sure about that?" Chaba's face split in an eerie grin. "Hit the back button on that video feed."

Cade's pulse bounced, but Chaba's steady gaze shot ice through him and with one eye on Chaba, he hit the speed rewind.

Images raced in backward, horrific motion as he saw one woman slam the other's head into the wall, then one of them holding a gun on the other, the women changing clothes.

"She was a little surprised to find I knew all about her little trick," Chaba said. "Of course, I told her I'd let her live if she brought the globe up. But my man has his orders. She won't be coming up—with the globe or without it."

Blood roared in Cade's ears. Sienna was set to die, and she was eighty feet down.

"You could go ahead and kill me," Chaba said as if reading Cade's racing thoughts, "but you've got only one spear and my Uzi isn't going to do you any good underwater. But since I found out weeks ago that you were on Valuatu Island, I've got a good idea how you got here. I know all about that little chemical you're so interested in. All my experimental patients, shall we say, died. I guess I shouldn't have given up so easily. Apparently it works, after all. I'll have to rededicate myself. Now you can go save your pretty friend, or you can stand here and keep talking to me. Your choice."

Run, baby, run!

He'd hesitated and Peter had died. His mother had died. All because of this evil man, and there was no hesitating now.

He roared as he took one blinding leap toward Chaba and slammed his fist into the man's jaw, cracking the terror leader backward against the bridge, where he left him sliding to the deck. Grabbing the Uzi, useless to him but not to Chaba if he woke up, he threw it in the sea and dove in after, praying.

If PAX was too late, if Chaba woke up and tried to escape, PAX was going to blow that boat out of the water before they'd let the terror leader escape. Then he'd never find out what was in that Valuatu bomb.

But if Cade was too late… Then none of the rest of it would really matter to him anymore.

Chaba's man tapped his dive watch, staring at her through the drenching blue, his gaze cold, assessing. Chaba had given her a time limit and she'd deliberately dragged his man on a wild-goose chase along the seabed, away from the hull, following the scattered trail of junk as if she were purposefully heading for something, then shaking her head, turning off to follow another wrong track. The diver stuck right by her side. The fantasy world of coral and fishes turned into a nightmare as time soaked on. Cade and his agency. She had to hang on, keep hanging on.

She shook her head violently again, waved her arm, signaling in another direction. *Don't panic, don't panic.* She was past panic. She could either produce the globe, or die. She knew that. Knew that they'd kill her even if she did find the globe.

Knew thousands of other people would die, too, if she gave it to Chaba.

The man's eyes narrowed with purpose inside his mask.

She kicked her feet and swam for her life, flashing sideways as the spear barreled past her, then he was on her, faster than her—something ripped from her back and struck her head. Her vision swam and confusion swamped her for an awful beat as she realized what he'd hit her with as she choked. He'd torn off her tank!

Fishes darted and light spun from overhead, flashing bits of sky through the dark water. He had an arm around her waist, the other tearing off her mask and air hose. She had no air! She struck out at his chest but he was nothing but hard rock and even harder eyes and she was holding her breath, suffocating.

Dizziness streaked through her. She kept fighting, struggled free, made it ten feet and he had her again. The disorientation waved over her in sick tides of pain.

Blood. So much blood!

Then her vision went black and she felt everything fall away, the pain, the cruel grip, even as a mouth crushed hers, breath slamming into her lungs.

Her heart stumbled as he let her go and breath held, she stared into Cade's hot, worried gaze. He gripped her cheeks in his hands, kissed her again, poured more life-giving air into her lungs and all she could do was throw her arms around him and hold him like she'd never let go. Because she never wanted to. She didn't know what had happened to Chaba or Sabrina or how he'd gotten there, but he was there. He was alive.

He tore away from her again, grabbed her hand and pointed up. Now her gaze spun and she saw him, the diver. Cade's spear straight through his neck, blood fanning out around him. Cade didn't give her time to absorb that horror. He pulled her, stopping once, twice, to make sure she had the air she needed.

The surface world was a nightmare she didn't recognize. Choppers streaked overhead. Chaba's boat raced across the water.

"Sabrina!" Sienna cried, grabbing onto Cade's shoulders. He tugged her into his arms as they saw the Sabrina's silhouette leap off the back of the boat and then— Fire shot in every direction as a missile from one of the choppers streaked down and the boat exploded.

Her heart crashed then she saw a basket, a man, lowering from a helicopter over Sabrina in the distance. Another chopper circled, headed back to Cade and Sienna.

"Oh, God," she whispered, choked. "Everything you told me about her—" Hot tears burst down her face even as her body felt cold and nearly numb. Then she saw the jagged, bleeding holes in Cade's shoulder and he was all that mattered. "Are you all right?"

"I'm fine. You're alive. I'm fine."

Aching, anguished thoughts roiled through her mind. "You're not fine. I know you're not fine."

"Go!" Cade said, pushing her toward the lowering basket. He kissed her hard. "Go! They're waiting for you. They're sending a team with boats, divers. They'll take care of the globe. You have to go."

"I know it's here, it's down there, inside that hull. I remembered— I didn't tell Chaba. I would never have told him! I was going to come back. I printed out the site map and—"

He nodded. "I know. Sienna, I know. Now go. You'll be safe now. You'll be—"

She'd die, that's what she'd do. He was sending her away. "No!" She grabbed hold of his good arm, not letting go. "Not without you. You said the team would take care of the globe. You're hurt. And I need you." Her voice cracked. "Please don't say goodbye."

The basket splashed down.

His ravaged gaze burned into her. "Don't make this harder than it—"

"Stop trying to save me!" she cried at him, wanting to beat her fists on his chest, anything. He was trying to protect her, still, and she didn't want to be protected, not from him. "It's the bark of the oratomu tree. It grows on Valuatu Island. I know about the secret chemical. Chaba told me." She watched his eyes shoot wide. "I told him it was the only way I'd bring up the globe. I knew he didn't even care—I knew he was planning to kill me whether I brought the globe up or not. I knew you would come." Her voice broke, and she let the last of the walls she'd hid behind tumble down. "And I knew I was the one who'd told the biggest lie of all when I said I wasn't falling in love with you. And if I hadn't reacted so stupidly this morning…"

Dark anguish crossed his face. "That wasn't your fault," he rasped, his voice rife with guilt. "That was mine. You were supposed to be the job and—" Emotion balled up his voice. "You don't want to love me. And I don't know how to love you. I'm a machine, that's what they call me."

"You're not a machine!" *Please, God, please.* She held on to him tightly, held on to that emotion threatening to spill out of him, that final truth she needed more than she needed to take her next breath. "You loved your family, you loved Peter. If you can't love me, that's one thing, but don't say you're a machine and can't love anyone, because I know that's not true."

"Sienna," he whispered roughly, taking her face into his hands. "He could have lied to you. Or it could be too late. There will have to be research, tests. There are no guarantees about what's next."

"I don't want a guarantee!" Her voice broke again. She was crying like a baby and she didn't care. "I want you." The man from the chopper was yelling at them from the basket bobbing toward them in the water.

She could barely breathe from her heart choking her throat. And she definitely couldn't see straight, because she would have sworn he was the one crying now, not her.

The chopper's rotors beat above them and her heart pounded like mad in her chest as she saw all those emotions he swore he didn't have written all over his face.

"I've never seen a machine cry," she said thickly. "Tell me you can forget me. Tell me you can't love me."

"I can't tell you that." The words tore from him, and he kissed her, kissed her hard and fast and hot, his tears mixing with hers. "I can't lie to you anymore," he whispered against her mouth. "I don't want to say goodbye."

"Then say hello," she whispered back. He held her tightly and she realized she was crying again. "Just say hello."

"Didn't we kind of skip that part in the beginning?" he asked, and even though they were both crying now, he looked as ridiculously happy as she felt. The sun splashed down around them, dancing light on the deep blue waves.

She nodded. "Let's start over." And they did.

Epilogue

Together they held hands and swam through the impossibly clear blue underworld, fishes and fans swaying out from the path. Cade could stay there forever, but he didn't have to, not anymore. The chemical treatment using the oratomu extract was working, allowing his body to adapt to longer and longer periods on the surface. One day at a time. Each one better than the last.

He wouldn't have to give up the surface world for an eternity under the sea. And that was damn good in his book, because an eternity in Sienna's bed sounded so much better.

She grinned at him now, stopping, pointing to the fairy-tale fantasy tilting up at them from the sea. A ship's hull, wrapped in candy-colored coral. She dipped down, brushed away at the sand, dug, came up with a gold doubloon.

He swam through the swirls of fish toward her, struck anew by the happiness she brought him, every day, every moment.

They'd spent months as part of the *Santa Josefa* excavation team. PAX had made Sienna part of the team—she'd been determined to do her part to bring up the globe and whatever other secrets the galleon held, breaking free of the past and her fears. She'd cleaned out her apartment in Raleigh, left everything behind to stick by him and what they'd started. She wasn't afraid of his future, no matter what it held.

And for the first time, he actually wanted a future. Chaba was dead. He couldn't hurt anyone ever again. Sabrina was in federal prison for the rest of her life, and the healing came one day at a time, for Sienna as well as for him.

He circled the Spanish galleon she'd found, scooped her into his arms and she lifted away her mask and the mouthpiece to her regulator and smiled. She held up the gold coin, then threw it over her shoulder, let it dance across the seabed and shook her head.

Her arms went around him, sweet possession, utter completeness, and he sank his lips onto hers, tasting her happiness, her love, his life. He was her treasure, and she was his.

They linked hands again and kept going.

Other people needed gold. They had each other.

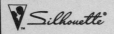

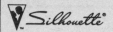
INTIMATE MOMENTS™

Psychic agent Eric Vinland's mission
to recover stolen government secrets
is jeopardized when his powers
disappear. Suddenly, he doesn't
know which is worse…being hunted
by fanatical terrorists, or his
vulnerability to the only woman
he's never been able to read,
partner Dawn Moon.

STRAIGHT
THROUGH
THE HEART

BY LYN STONE

**Silhouette Intimate Moments
#1408**

**AVAILABLE MARCH 2006
AT YOUR FAVORITE RETAIL OUTLET.**

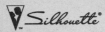

passionate powerful provocative love stories

Silhouette Desire delivers strong heroes, spirited heroines and compelling love stories.

Desire features your favorite authors, including

Annette Broadrick, Ann Major, Anne McAllister and Cait London.

Passionate, powerful and provocative romances *guaranteed!*

For superlative authors, sensual stories and sexy heroes, choose Silhouette Desire.

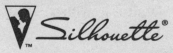

passionate powerful provocative love stories

BOUNTY HUNTER.
HEIRESS.
CHANTAL WORTHINGTON WAS

HELL ON HEELS

by Carla CASSIDY

Chantal was on familiar terrain
when she went after a fellow blue blood
who'd skipped bail on a rape charge.
But teaming up with bounty hunter
Luke Coleman to give chase was a
new move in her playbook. Soon things
were heating up on—and off—the case....

Available March 2006

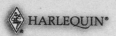

HARLEQUIN®

INTRIGUE

Don't miss this first title in Lori L. Harris's
exciting new Harlequin Intrigue series—

THE BLADE BROTHERS
OF COUGAR COUNTY

TARGETED

(Harlequin Intrigue #901)

BY **LORI L. HARRIS**

On sale February 2006

Alec Blade and Katie Carroll think they can start
fresh in Cougar County. Each hopes to bury the
unresolved events of their violent pasts. But they
soon learn just how mistaken they are when a
faceless menace reappears in their lives. Suddenly
it isn't a matter of outrunning the past. Now they
have to survive long enough to have a future.

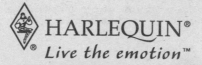

HARLEQUIN®
Live the emotion™

COMING NEXT MONTH

#1407 A HUSBAND'S WATCH—Karen Templeton
The Men of Mayes County
After a tornado destroys mechanic Darryl Andrew's garage,
he realizes that more than a broken arm and livelihood need
rebuilding—his marriage is in serious danger of crumbling. While
Darryl's secrets continue to plague their relationship,
Faith Meyerhauser is torn between her loyalty to her husband and
family and following a dream she's buried for nearly
twelve years.

#1408 STRAIGHT THROUGH THE HEART—Lyn Stone
Special Ops
NSA agent Dawn Moon is chosen to assist Eric Vinland, the
sexy agent whose psychic abilities are crucial in recovering stolen
government secrets. But the mission is put in jeopardy when Eric
realizes his powers have disappeared, and he doesn't know which
is worse…being hunted down by a group of terrorists, or his
vulnerability to the only woman he's never
been able to read.

#1409 MEMORIES AFTER MIDNIGHT—
Linda Randall Wisdom
When Alexandra Spencer is attacked in a seemingly random
mugging, a head injury causes her to forget her divorce from the
one man who can save her—police detective Dylan Parker. Dylan
senses there is more to the crime and reluctantly takes up the
investigation, but finds it hard to concentrate as he is drawn to
the kinder, gentler woman who still sparks his desires.

#1410 THE ARSONIST—Mary Burton
Reporter Darcy Sampson is convinced a serial arsonist is
still alive, and she seeks out former arson investigator
Michael Gannon for answers. When fires erupt in Darcy's
hometown, the two must battle to solve the case and the attraction
threatening to consume them both.

SIMCNM0206